THE STAGE FROM DEADWOOD

AN EVANS NOVEL OF THE WEST

THE STAGE FROM DEADWOOD

RAY TOEPFER

M. EVANS AND COMPANY, INC.
NEW YORK

M. Evans and Company, Inc.
216 East 49th Street
New York, New York 10017

Library of Congress Cataloguing-in-Publication Data

Toepfer, Ray Grant.
    The Stage from Deadwood/Ray Toepfer
        p.   cm. — (An Evans novel of the West)
    ISBN 0-87131-743-5 (cloth) : $18.95
    I. Title.   II. Series.
PS3570.O415S7   1993
813'.54—dc20   39-24524
                                                                        CIP

Typeset by Classic Type, Inc.

Manufactured in the United States of America

9 8 7 6 5 4 3 2 1

For
Rhonda
and
Jesse
and
Erika

Chapter One

Everybody called him Colonel, although it was pretty obvious to Charlie Pearse that Reynolds hadn't been an officer. He most likely had been a sergeant in the war or maybe afterward. He didn't carry himself the way most people figured an officer would, with a ramrod down his back, but he got the name because he could tell you which general had made what mistake in which battle.

Of course the war was fifteen years behind them now, and the ones who had been in it were generally happy to forget the experience, and the ones like Charlie Pearse were too young to care. The Union had been saved, and folks were getting around to allowing as how the South hadn't been all bad, and as how not every Yankee was a money-grubbing skinflint. You could even find a Yank and a Reb sharing drinks at the bar or doing their fighting over a hand of poker.

Colonel Reynolds' last name could have been either Yank or Reb, and he stood six feet without boots, which was six inches taller than Charlie Pearse. He had good muscle that showed he'd done some heavy physical labor somewhere along the line, and he hadn't let it run to fat, the way some did. He liked a drink now and then, and he played a little poker, but mostly he took care of his business, which was running the best livery stable in Julesburg, Colorado. He charged fair prices, he had two good hostlers to take care of the horses and tack, and he occasionally rented out his two fancy buggies to young sparks out courting.

He was in Dick Martin's saloon the night Charlie had a problem with Billy Kenyon, and it gave him an idea as to how Charlie could handle himself.

Billy was drunk, and he left the bar to stand behind Charlie's chair. Charlie was a professional gambler, which meant that he didn't cheat, he played a good game and generally won, and he didn't want anybody standing behind him and looking at his cards so they could tip off the other players.

"Get away from there, Billy," Charlie said politely. "It's bad manners to stand behind somebody's chair."

"I'm watching."

"Not from there, you're not. Move."

"Make me," Billy said.

"If you'll excuse me, gents. I got some business to take care of." Charlie pushed his chair away from the table and put his cards in his pocket, and then he stood up.

Billy Kenyon was even taller than Colonel, and he weighed two-fifty to Charlie's one hundred and fifty pounds, and there wasn't any doubt in Colonel's mind that Charlie Pearse was about to get his plow cleaned. Billy wasn't noted for following Marquis of Queensbury rules.

Colonel also knew that "Poker" Pearse had a reputation of being a fast man with a gun, and he raced the other three players away from the table to get out of the line of fire.

Billy lowered his head, pulled his right arm back, and then he rushed in for the kill. One good punch would take out Charlie, and then he could work him over to his heart's content. It didn't happen. Charlie stood there, one foot ahead of the other, arms hanging loose at the elbows, and when Billy Kenyon came in, Charlie spun on his feet, grabbed Billy by the right wrist and the right upper arm and helped him along. Billy's feet went out from under him, and he slid six feet down the floor before he came to a stop.

He had splinters in his hands, and his face wouldn't have won a beauty prize, but he got up full of fight. Just in time to get Charlie's boot in the chest. He sat back down on the floor huffing and puffing like a locomotive going up a grade.

"You had about enough?" Charlie asked.

Billy rocked back and forth, and then he pushed himself to his feet. He stumbled forward getting up momentum, and when he figured he had enough to pulverize Charlie, he came in.

This time Charlie didn't spin aside. He brushed inside Billy's right arm, which was about as big as a normal man's thigh, and he hit Billy three right jabs to the solar plexus. Billy was still standing, but his eyes were out of focus and his face was turning blue.

"Water," Charlie said, and the bartender handed him a full pitcher to pour over Billy Kenyon.

Billy came back by slow degrees, but the fight was out of him. "What happened?" he mumbled.

"You must have tripped over something," Charlie said. To his credit, he didn't crack a smile.

Billy Kenyon finally got up. Without bothering to look around, he headed for the door, and a moment later they heard him being sick in the street. "I never saw anything quite like that," Colonel said.

"A trick I learned from a bartender back in Kansas," Charlie said as he took his cards from his pocket. "Now, can we play cards?"

It was a good night for Charlie. He came out fifty-two dollars ahead, ten of which went to Dick Martin for the table, and another five for his share of the winnings.

The other three players drifted off into the night, and Charlie poured drinks for Colonel and himself from the bottle he'd bought for the table. He waited for Colonel to say what he was going to say. It wasn't long in coming.

"I heard you were a fast man with a gun, Charlie. Soon as you hit town, word got out. They were saying you were the fastest draw since Bill Hickock."

"No way of proving that, Colonel. Hickok's been dead for four years now."

"Seventy-six, wasn't it? Four years is a long time." Colonel gave him an unexpected grin. "I got a little matter I'd like you to handle for me."

"I'm not a hired gun, Colonel. I don't shoot unless I have to, and it's surely not for money."

Colonel nodded. "You'll do. I need somebody who can handle himself. Somebody I can trust. I figure you're an honest man. I've seen you play cards and you don't cheat. I saw you throw a man out of the game when he did, and you didn't use a gun then either. Like tonight."

"All of it called for," Charlie said. "I never killed a man who wasn't trying to kill me first."

"If you're interested in a little job on the side, take you maybe a week, come around to the stable tomorrow."

Charlie Pearse nodded. "I'll listen, but that's all I can promise until I hear more."

Colonel raised his glass. "That's fair enough. I'll see you in the morning, then."

When Colonel had left, Dick Martin came in from the back door to close up. "That was some fight," he said. "I seen it from the back door. You're plumb full of surprises, Charlie. I seen you throw a man out before, but not one twice your size."

Charlie settled with Dick, and then walked down the street to his hotel and climbed the stairs to his room on the top floor.

It was the early summer of 1880, and already it was hot in the daytime, although it cooled down considerably at night. Even so, Pearse's room was hot most of the night because the building next to it blocked off the breeze from the west. It was cool enough by two or three in the morning, when Pearse generally went to bed, and it stayed cool until ten or eleven in the morning, when he usually got up.

He got up at nine the morning after the fight. He was curious about Colonel's proposition, and he wanted to get some breakfast before he talked to the man. Not that he mistrusted Colonel, but he had learned to be cagey when it came to easy money.

He went down the street to the cafe and had a good breakfast. Pearse was partial to a small steak and eggs and pancakes, with lots of good coffee to wash it down. He didn't even have to give an order: the waitress knew what he wanted and brought it over as soon as he settled down.

He took his time eating, because he wanted to think about what Colonel wanted him to do for him and what he was going to tell him in case it was something Pearse didn't want to do. He was not going to get on the wrong side of the law for him, that was certain. He was not going to kill anybody for him or steal money or anything stupid. On the other hand, he couldn't see Colonel asking him to do anything of that sort. He was man enough to do his own killing, if that was what he had in mind, and he didn't need any more money than he had.

That left Pearse back where he started, so he finished his fourth cup of coffee and walked down the street to Colonel's livery stable.

Josh White, the head hostler, was cleaning out a stall when Pearse walked in. He nodded to the office in back. "He's waiting for you, Charlie."

Pearse winked at him and walked down the long alley past the rumps of assorted bays and roans and paints and calicos until he got to the boxed-in stall Colonel used for an office.

"Morning, Colonel. You look bright-eyed and bushy-tailed for a man's been playing poker untll two o'clock."

"Morning to you, Charlie." He waved Pearse to a chair.

They lit ritual cigars and Colonel offered him a glass of whiskey, which Pearse turned down. Morning was not the time to start drinking, and this was not the place.

Colonel reached in his pocket and pulled out a telegram flimsy. "I got this yesterday morning. Read it."

"John dead. Waiting at hotel for your help. Nest egg safe. Mary Lou." The clerk's neat copperplate seemed to dispel the sense of urgency. Pearse read the telegram twice and passed it back.

"Who's Mary Lou and why does she need help?" he asked.

"It's a long story, Charlie. Her father and I were partners in the sutlery up at Fort Robinson. Mary Lou and I were to be married this month, and she was escorted from the fort by John Logan, a friend of mine. He was First Sergeant with thirty years in, and he was discharged up there this week. Mary Lou's father died last month, and she put the money from the sale of the sutlery and my profits in a letter of credit which she was to deposit in the Deadwood bank. If John is gone, I need somebody to escort Mary Lou down here, and I need somebody I can trust to bring the money here as well."

"What happened to John Logan?"

"The Lord only knows," Colonel said. "He wasn't the flighty kind, and I'd have trusted him with my life. Hell, I did a coupleof times in the Indian troubles. But something's gone wrong up there, and Mary Lou says she needs help. John was going to bring her down here, and now he can't. That's reason enough for me."

Pearse nodded. "I can see where there's reason to worry. Did Logan know about the money?"

"I don't think so. I didn't tell him."

"Is the money in the bank up there?"

Colonel shrugged. "I'd guess. She said the nest-egg was safe, and we agreed that she'd put the letter in the bank as soon as she got there. That means it's in the bank."

Pearse thought about it. "So you want me to escort the lady down here."

"And pick up the money at the bank and bring it down too."

"I'm going to ask a dumb question. What's keeping you from going up there yourself?"

Colonel smiled. "It's not dumb, Charlie. There's a man who'd give his eyeteeth to kill me, and if I showed my face in Deadwood, he'd know for certain about the money. He broke out of prison a month ago, and I'm pretty sure he's up there somewhere in that area. I don't want to put Mary Lou in any more danger than she's in already."

"Won't she be in danger anyway?"

Colonel shook his head. "I don't know, Charlie. I just don't know. That's why I need you up there."

Why me? Why did this man I know only slightly pick me? Pearse thought. He asked.

"I hear a lot of things in here, Charlie. I heard about how you got the man was shooting Jim Thatcher's stock last summer. Jim told me about it, and I must say I got a lot of respect for a man of your ability."

"You over-rate me, Colonel," Pearse said. "I did about what I had to do, and I didn't like doing some of it."

"No man would." Colonel laid his cigar in a saucer and hunched forward. "You're the right man for the job, Charlie. You're honest and you can handle yourself with or without a gun. I saw that last night."

Pearse had another question. "Why can't I get a letter of credit to the bank here in Julesburg? Be a lot safer than carrying cash."

"I don't want Julesburg to know about it. I've got investments in the fire that won't wait more than a week, and if word got out that I had money in the bank, it would cost me twice as much. If I can put cash on the barrelhead, I'll make money. If I don't, I'll lose it. I know it's risky to escort a lady and carry a bunch of cash, but it's the only way I can see to handle it. It was safe enough with John Logan handling it. Besides, a letter of credit can be stolen too. Forgery isn't beyond a scheming man, as I'm sure you know."

"I know. But it's a lot of responsibility to put on a fellow. Escort a lady and carry a bunch of cash money to boot."

Colonel nodded. "I've thought of that, Charlie."

At twenty-four, Charlie Pearse's world was his oyster. There was nothing he thought he couldn't do. But he didn't necessarily have to do it Colonel's way. "How would you want me to work it?"

"That would depend upon what you found up there. I'd say take the stage, except that Josh heard a couple of riders talking about a gold shipment coming down from Deadwood. If that shipment was on the stage you were taking, you might be in for trouble. The men Josh heard were acting like they had something in mind, like holding up the stage."

"I don't know how I'd handle that, Colonel. Except maybe wait for another stage. Always assuming that I could pick one without a gold shipment."

Colonel nodded. "I've thought about that. If you had to, you could always ride in on horseback. Mary Lou's a good horsewoman. Hell, I taught her myself. Her daddy and me taught her how to handle a gun too."

Pearse decided. If John Logan had handled it, so could Charlie Pearse. "Done, Colonel. When do I start?"

"As soon as you can. You have to leave here without anybody knowing when you're leaving or where you're going. And you're going to have to keep all this to yourself. Don't trust a soul. If you can, find out what happened to John Logan, but don't waste time doing it. John was a good man, but he's dead now, and there's not a thing you can do about it."

Pearse nodded. He could always think up a story to cover his absence. "I'll do my best, Colonel. But if I can't handle the lady and the money both, I take it you want me to leave the money up there and bring down the lady. Right?"

"Right. It's worth a thousand dollars to me to have you do the job. If you have to buy horses or anything, I'll reimburse you for it. The thousand is to cover the time you'll lose playing poker. Maybe it'll take care of some of those nights when the cards don't run your way."

They shook hands on the deal, and then Colonel penned a note to the Deadwood bank and signed it. "This'll get you the cash," he said. "From here on out, it's up to you."

"How about the lady? Doesn't she need to know me?"

"I can send a telegram," Colonel said.

"Can you trust the operator here?"

Colonel stared at him. "I'll make it complicated for him. 'Help on way. Charlie.' How's that?"

Pearse grinned. "You think of everything, don't you?"

"I try to."

"I'll have to explain to Dick Martin I'll be gone, but if I leave tomorrow, I ought to be there by Wednesday."

"The sooner the better," Colonel said.

When Charlie Pearse walked out, Colonel stubbed out his cigar. He'd made the right choice. Charlie Pearse was known as a man of his word. If he said he could do it, he would.

Colonel had made up his mind to ask Pearse to handle it for him before the fight in the saloon last night. He had talked with various people around town, the sheriff included, and they all seemed to have a good opinion of Poker Pearse. He hadn't, of course, told anybody that he was thinking of asking Pearse to do a job for him. That would have given the whole show away, and he couldn't afford to do that. But what he heard, especially from Sheriff Carrington, was good.

Pearse had an interesting history, for a man not yet twenty-five. He had been orphaned early in life, and his half-brother had cheated him royally, hiring him for peanuts to run his general store for him. Finally, Pearse had left town and begun to learn to make his way as a man. He had a natural gift for arithmetic, and he had learned to play poker like an expert. He had also learned plainscraft from an ex-gunslinger who ran a saloon in his home town, Caliope, Kansas. Hell of a name, the Colonel thought.

One way or another, Charlie Pearse had wound up in Caliope again, running from three outlaws who wanted his money and his life. He had prudently tried to avoid a showdown, but when it came, according to Carrington, he had killed three men. Caliope was pretty much tamed after that.

"He came out here then," Carrington had said. "He worked for Jim Thatcher over on the JT, and when somebody tried to kill Miz Thatcher, he finally got the fellow. Make no mistake, Charlie Pearse is quick with a deck of cards, but he's even quicker with a gun. Carries one of them Starr self-cockers. That and an old Sharps buffalo gun. He's good with both."

The impression of Poker Pearse that Colonel got was of a man who'd been a loner for most of his life. A man who could handle himself in almost any situation. A man who was fair and honest and who couldn't be bought. And when the chips were down, a man who could fight with his fists or with a gun.

Colonel respected that.

Chapter Two

While it was all fresh in his mind, Pearse went back to his room and got out a sheet of paper and his pen and ink. He wrote down everything Colonel had told him and stated his mission. It wouldn't hurt to have a backup plan, in case he got in too deep to get out by himself. When he had finished, he read what he'd written, made a couple of corrections, and folded the paper in thirds, sealing it with candle wax and addressing it to Sheriff Carrington. Then he walked down the street to the sheriff's office.

Colonel had explained why he was sending Charlie to fetch his bride-to-be and his money, and Pearse guessed it was good enough to satisfy the Colonel. It wasn't the way he would have handled it, that was for sure. He would have gone up there and got his girl himself, and devil take the man who tried to stand in his way. As far as the money was concerned, he would have left it there until it was safe, deal or no deal.

But that was the way Colonel wanted it. Maybe that was what it was like to be forty instead of twenty-four.

"I'd like you to hold this for me, Sheriff."

"What do I do with it?"

Pearse smiled. "Just hold it. If I'm not back, in say two weeks, read it. Then you can get somebody to go out and start looking for me, because I'll be needing help."

Carrington frowned and lit up a stogie. "You sound like you might be into something too big for you to handle."

"I don't think so. It's only insurance. But if I'm wrong, you'll know what to do."

Carrington puffed blue smoke at the wall. "You're the boss, Charlie. I just hope to hell I don't have to open this."

"That makes two of us."

When he left the sheriff's office, Pearse headed for Dick Martin's saloon. As he walked, he speculated on what had happened to John Logan. Was his death an accident? Or was it tied in to the money? If it was, Pearse was in trouble the minute he set foot in Deadwood.

He told Dick Martin that he had to go to Kansas on family business. It was as good a story as any.

"Going to be gone long?" Dick asked.

"Hard telling. I ought to be back in a week, but you know how family business is. It can drag on."

"You get a letter from somebody?"

"No. It's old business, but things are a little slow, and I figured I'd better take care of it."

"All right, we'll make out. I'll hold a table for you.

There was a stage from Julesburg to North Platte: it was the easiest way to get to Caliope, Kansas. But he would have to backtrack to get up to Deadwood and there wasn't time. The best bet was to ride out of Julesburg and then cut north to Deadwood.

Pearse put on riding clothes and packed his good suit in a saddle bag. Then he went down to the livery stable and got out the bay gelding he'd bought last fall. Colonel watched him. "Going someplace, Charlie?"

For the benefit of the stable hands, Pearse said, "Got to go to Kansas on family business, Colonel."

"Hope it's nothing serious."

Now Colonel knew he was riding out instead of taking the stage, but there wasn't much he could do about that. Pearse had no good reason to mistrust the man, but he'd learned over the years that if you had something you needed to do, the fewer people who knew about it, the better off you were.

Inside of an hour, he guessed, all Julesburg would know when he left and what horse he was riding. But there was something he could do about that. Not that it mattered now, but he didn't want to be identified the minute he set foot in Deadwood.

He had his Big Fifty Sharps with him, all ten pounds of it, and forty rounds. His .44-40 Starr self-cocker was in the other saddlebag, and he had plenty of ammunition for that too. He also had some plans of his own that didn't include Colonel.

For openers, taking a lady and a large sum of money on a stagecoach was a damn fool thing to do. Stages got held up, and then he'd have to worry about protecting the lady and the money both. Two things to worry about instead of one. But if he got another horse and set out across country with Mary Lou and the money, he'd stand a better chance of making it in one piece. Once again he was relying on his instinct: the fewer people who knew what he was going to do, the safer he and the lady would be.

Pearse pulled up about ten miles from town and sat in a little thicket near a creek and watched his back trail for half an hour. If anybody was planning to bushwhack him, they'd probably wait until he got to Deadwood. But if he came in on a horse they didn't know and from a different direction, he'd have a slight advantage.

When he had waited long enough to spot anybody coming up behind him, he turned north to the JT, where he and Jim Thatcher had gone through a hard winter a year ago.

Thatcher was glad to see him. "What brings you out this way, Charlie?"

"I need a favor."

A tall, lean man of forty, Thatcher was a typical rancher. He had built a herd from scratch, and he was in the position of having done well and on the verge of doing better. He nodded to Charlie. "Come on in and have a cup of coffee, and tell me about it."

Pearse wanted a different horse. A stayer, he said, and he wanted a Winchester saddle gun. "I'll leave my horse here and that big Sharps. I want to go someplace where I don't want the whole town to know Charlie Pearse is riding in."

"No problem at all, Charlie. You can pick the horse, and I got a saddle gun ought to suit you. It's .44-40, so you can use the same shells you use in your Starr." Thatcher sipped at his coffee. "Sounds like you're expecting trouble."

"Let's say I want to be ready for it if it comes."

He tried out a dun gelding and the Winchester, and they both seemed fine. He offered Thatcher money for the loan, but Thatcher would have none of it. "What are friends for?"

Pearse thanked him and headed north. He had three days' hard riding ahead, and it was time to get on with it.

He made about thirty miles that night before he stopped in a little ravine close to a ranch they'd examined the year before. He spent the first hour watching his back trail until it was too dark to see, and once during the night he got up and looked to the south to see if somebody had lit a campfire. There was nothing, and he went back to sleep until the dawn mist awakened him.

Pearse was making up his plans as he rode, on the sound assumption that if he didn't know what he was going to do next, nobody else would either. The best way to go would be to ride north and come into Deadwood from the east. He guessed he could make a hundred and fifty miles in three days.

There was nothing outstanding about the second day on the trail either. Nobody was following him that he could see, and he was making good time. But he had a nagging suspicion that there was a leak of information and that it came from Julesburg. Somebody had known about John Logan, maybe about the letter of credit too, and however it had happened, John Logan was dead.

He camped out on a bare space on the far side of a hill, eating cold bacon and hardtack, and staying warm enough in his blankets without a fire.

But the dun was showing signs of strain, and Pearse was glad when he came to a stage station late in the afternoon. He thought it would have been nice to say he'd been smart enough to know it was there, but he had to admit that it was pure dumb luck that he'd found it. He rode up and gave the station master a story about getting lost and how he had to get to Lead to meet his partner, who was foreman in a mine.

"You could leave your horse here for a dollar a day," the agent offered.

Pearse pretended to think about it. "The only trouble with that is, I'm not sure when I'll be back. And I'll need a horse up there."

"Tell you what," the agent said. "There's a stage coming through in about an hour bound for Rapid City and Deadwood. If the driver's willing to let you tie your horse on behind, your troubles are over. You want something to eat?"

Pearse sat down behind a plank table supported on kegs and tucked into a meal of stringy boiled beef, potatoes, and underbaked bread. He paid a dollar for it, but at least it was hot, and the station master's wife refilled it for free.

The stage pulled in two hours later, and the passengers got off to eat while the team was changed and the coach wheels inspected for cracked spokes or loose rims. Pearse strolled over to talk to the driver.

He was a small, hard-bitten man in his forties, and he looked as if he had a perpetual gripe. "Damn nuisance taking a horse on behind," he said. "But if he can keep up, I guess it'll be all right."

Pearse threw his saddle and bedroll on top of the stage and lashed them down with his rope, and then he got up beside the driver. There was no shotgun riding this stage, and Pearse asked about it.

"Takes up room a passenger could fill. And there ain't nothing worth stealing except what the passengers got on them."

That was one way of putting it. Pearse could see from the driver's ratty clothes that he was on the downhill side of his job. A top driver dressed the part. His clothes were neat and his boots were clean, if not polished. He minded his manners, especially around ladies, and he was friendly. A good driver wouldn't be on this run, though. He'd be on an important run, like the one from Deadwood down to Cheyenne.

A smart fellow could see the handwriting on the wall, of course. In another five or ten years, the stage coach would be a thing of the past, driven out by the railroads. The only stages left running would be the ones that ran north or south from an inland town to one on the railroad. The trains had already taken over most of the east-west traffic, except for lightly traveled routes like this, and it was only a matter of time before they'd have that sewed up too.

They started off with a rattle and a jangle, and the big wheels cut wide tracks in the dust. It got cold when the sun went down, but the dirt still came up from the hooves of the six-horse team and settled in a fine stream over the coach and its passengers. Pearse could smell sage in the night, and there was enough light from the stars to see the trail and the low hills that seemed to get steeper the further they went.

At the top of one hill the driver pulled up to rest the horses. He got down from the box and went alongside the team, examining each horse with a practiced eye.

"You got a gun handy?" he asked when he pulled himself back onto the seat. "Somebody's up ahead."

Pearse stood on the box and hauled out the rifle from his saddle scabbard. "This good enough?"

"Fine. They don't run a shotgun any more. I got me a Colt, but it's always better if there's two men up here."

Pearse looked back at the dun. It looked to be in good shape; he'd watered it and put a nosebag on at the last stop.

They went down the hill a good deal faster than they'd come up, and they got a good run at the next hill. At the top a man stood in the trail and hailed them. Pearse kept the Winchester ready, and the driver had his Colt in his lap. For all his talk, he wasn't taking chances, and Pearse got a little more respect for him.

"I need a ride to Deadwood," the man said. "My horse broke a leg and I had to shoot him."

"Sure," the driver said. "Throw your saddle up top and climb aboard. Only three others in there."

Pearse got a look at the man as he came around to throw his tack up to the top of the coach. He was maybe six foot, but not heavy. He was leaned out like a man who'd done some work in his day, but he wasn't dressed like a working man. Or like a rider, for that matter. He had dark pants on and fine calfskin boots, and he wore a respectable alpaca coat and a good flat-crowned hat. He looked like a preacher or a gambling man, and Pearse wondered what he was doing out in the middle of Dakota territory. The more he wondered, the less he liked it. Anything out of the ordinary was suspicious, and this was decidedly out of the ordinary.

The door slammed and the driver started the team on the downhill slope. The stage careened down toward a little dry stream-bed, and the wheels crunched through the pebbles before they bit the dirt of the slope beyond.

Chapter Three

They pulled into Rapid City at midnight. Deadwood was the next stop, but Pearse had had enough. He was bone-weary, the dun looked more dead than alive, and there was no sense arriving in Deadwood at three in the morning.

He made arrangements with the stage agent to keep his horse, and then he walked down the street to a small frame building that pretended to be a hotel. It wasn't great shucks by Julesburg standards, but it was reasonably clean. It was also five dollars a night. Rapid City was a boom town.

Pearse didn't make it out of bed until noon, and nobody bothered him. He found a place that served passable food, and then he went down to the stage office and looked the dun over. He had benefitted from the rest and a good bait of oats. Pearse decided to ride on to Deadwood and stay there for the night.

There was something about a boom town that got under his skin. It was the stink of the place, he guessed. Not only the stink of a lot of people in one place without adequate bathing facilities or room to move around comfortably, but the stink of greed. Everybody was out to make a dollar, never mind how. For everybody who did there were ten more who didn't and probably never would.

Pearse rode into the hills, past burrows where solitary miners looked for gold or silver or whatever came along. Some were trying to get a living out of their holes, but most of them were trying to sell their claims and move on to richer diggings. Everybody was trying to make a dollar.

Tall lodgepole pines covered the slopes, and Pearse remembered that only ten years ago this had been off-limits to white men. It was sacred territory to the Sioux, and the first whites to come in after Custer's expedition in '74 called the area the Black Hills. The Indian name, Sapapa, sounded prettier.

He headed for Deadwood by slow degrees, stopping often and walking up the steeper hills to spare the dun. Even though the Sioux had been pacified and put on a reservation after Custer's battle at the Little Big Horn, there was still tension in the air. Suppose some of the Sioux hadn't quit? Suppose some miner who hadn't struck it rich with a shovel wanted to try a gun?

Pearse stopped just out of sight of town and strapped on his gunbelt. It never did anybody any harm to look like he was ready for anything. He'd learned that lesson a long time ago.

Pearse got into Deadwood about eight in the evening, and it was about the way he'd remembered it from three years back, when he'd lost his shirt in a crooked game. Like any boom town, Deadwood was full of unsavory characters, and Pearse knew enough to steer clear of them.

He stabled the horse at a livery stable on the edge of town, and then he walked down to a rooming house that didn't look like a hot bed place. That was what they called a place that slept you by shifts: one shift got up, the next one rolled in the sack, and the third one came in to turn the second one out. A person who owned a bed-and-board house and slept his tenants in three shifts could make a pile of money in no time.

Even though Pearse had come in on horseback and broken his trail at Rapid City, he had the feeling that he was being watched. A strictly logical person would have reasoned that he couldn't be followed, because nobody could be smart enough to follow him. But Pearse believed in hunches. He didn't believe that the man who had boarded the stage last night was unaware that Pearse might be on it.

When you thought that way, you looked for reasons, and the best reason Pearse could come up with was that somebody in

Julesburg had talked. Somebody would have said, Charlie Pearse went to see Colonel, and right after that he rode out headed east. But Colonel wouldn't have any business in the east. If Charlie was working for Colonel, he'd be headed for Deadwood, where Colonel had interests. If he also had an idea that those interests included money, he would take great notice of Charlie's doings.

The next morning Pearse washed and shaved and put on his good suit of clothes and headed out to tend to his business. He figured that his first act would be to find the lady, so he went down to the hotel where he'd stayed three years before and asked the clerk for her room number.

A good-looking lady answered the knock. "I'm Mary Lou Reilly," she said. "And you must be Charlie Pearse."

She was about thirty-five, a little younger than Colonel, and about ten years older than Pearse. slim and wiry, and she had pretty auburn hair that reminded Pearse of June Shelton's, the girl Charlie had hoped to marry.

But that was where the resemblance ended. Mary Lou Reilly had blue eyes, not brown, and her mouth was on the thin side. She looked like a lady who knew her business and who could take care of it without help, thank you kindly.

"Done looking, Mr. Pearse?" she asked tartly.

"Yes, ma'am," he smiled. "Have you eaten yet?"

"Early and often, like they say."

"I have a little business to transact, and then we can get started."

She looked at a little lapel watch. "It's ten o'clock now," she said. "The Cheyenne stage leaves at one."

"I'll come back for you in plenty of time," Pearse said. "And I want to check out that stage before we take it."

"Colonel said you were cagey. I'll see you shortly."

As Pearse walked down the stairs, he reviewed his impression of her. She was wearing a riding skirt and soft calfskin boots, so she was ready for anything. There were deep pockets in the skirt, and the one on the right side hung low. Pearse guessed that she had an equalizer in there. A woman traveling alone would be smart to carry a pistol, and this lady looked as if she had plenty of brains.

The only thing was, she didn't look like the kind of woman Colonel would pick to be his wife. She was a little hard around the edges, and he didn't think Colonel would get along with somebody who'd give him an argument.

And then it came to him that Colonel wouldn't have had time to send a wire to Mary Lou Reilly. Not in time to mention his name. He might have sent her a wire saying somebody would meet her, but he couldn't have known that Charlie Pearse would take the job.

It could have happened, of course, but it was something to think about. Until he knew her better, Mary Lou Reilly would bear some watching.

Pearse walked down to the stage office to check out the schedule. Sure enough, the Cheyenne stage left at one. Pearse told the agent that he hadn't quite made up his mind, and then he walked back up the street to the Deadwood bank. It hadn't been there in '77, when he'd last sampled the pleasures of Deadwood, but like most banks it gave the impression of having been around since Creation.

The man Pearse needed to see kept him waiting for fifteen minutes, but when he was finally free, he was pleasant enough. He took Pearse to a little cubbyhole partitioned off from the main lobby, and then he sent a clerk to the vault. The clerk came back with a black leather satchel tagged to Reynolds, and Pearse opened it and counted the money, all twenty thousand dollars.

It was a lot of money, by anybody's standards, and Pearse wondered why the satchel didn't have a lock. It looked like a doctor's bag, and that wouldn't have a lock either, but it was a hell of a lot of money to be toting around in a town like Deadwood.

"Got a lock for this?" Pearse asked.

"We've got one we could sell you," the banker said. "Fits around the handles. A dollar and fifty cents."

Pearse dug in his pocket. "Better safe than sorry," he said.

While the clerk went in search of the padlock and the banker made out a receipt for the money, Pearse thought about the black satchel. It would fit in a saddlebag easily enough, and it didn't weigh much. But if anybody got a look at it, it fairly advertised what it contained.

Pearse stuck the key to the padlock in his boot and signed the receipt for the money. There was nothing much he could do about the satchel. Not now, at any rate.

Before he left the bank, he put the satchel in a saddlebag, and then he walked out as if he hadn't a care in the world.

And then he got the first jolt of the day: across the street from the bank, propped against a hitching rail, was the gent who'd boarded the stage last night. He looked like a casual onlooker this morning, but Pearse didn't believe in coincidence. He was watching Pearse to see what Pearse looked like in daylight, and to make sure Pearse had remembered to go to the bank.

There was nothing to do but play out the game, Pearse decided. He went to the hotel and collected Mary Lou Reilly, and they walked down the street to the stage station. He carried his saddlebag over his left shoulder, she carried her carpetbag in her left hand. "In this town, you want your right hand free," she said, and Pearse thought he had just learned something else about her.

"There's going to be two stages for Cheyenne today," the agent announced. "One o'clock for the first one, two o'clock for the second."

Pearse guessed that one would be a bullion run, carrying gold to Cheyenne for transhipment to Denver by rail. The other would be a dummy. He asked the agent.

"I wouldn't know about that," the man said. "But Sam Bass and his gang used to hold up the stages pretty regular here about three years back, and the money men got cagey. It could be like you say, but I couldn't tell you even if I knew."

Pearse told him he understood, and then he bought a ticket for Mary Lou Reilly.

"I'll be riding on behind," he explained. "I have a horse belongs to a friend I got to return." He turned to the agent. "You got a place where I can change clothes?"

"The privy's out back. You can change in there."

Mary Lou Reilly looked down her nose. "Surely you're dressed well enough for riding?"

"Too well. This is my only good suit."

The malodorous privy had everything he needed: a good-sized stack of newspapers. Pearse got into his travel clothes, canvas pants, and a flannel shirt, and then he set to work cutting newspapers into bill-sized strips. When he finished, he dumped out his flour and bacon and coffee and put the currency from the satchel into the saddle bag. Then he put the newsprint into the black satchel, making sure to snap the lock around the handles.

"You took long enough," Mary Lou Reilly said. "It's almost time for the stage."

"Maybe we won't be taking that one," Pearse said.

"Scared?"

"Cautious," Pearse grinned. And then he remembered. "Do you know a man about six foot tall, dark hair, speaks like a gentleman, wears good clothes?"

"Why do you ask?"

"Somebody was awful curious about my trip to the bank this morning. He got on the same stage I was on last night, and he was across the street from the bank when I came out."

"It could be someone I used to know," she said cautiously. "But I don't know how he'd know I was here."

"It kind of bothers me."

"I can see where it would. I know about the money, by the way, so you don't have to pussyfoot around."

Pearse gave her his country-boy grin, the one that said, I've got nothing to hide and I'm just a likeable fellow trying to get along in this cruel world. "What money was that?"

"Why the twenty thousand dollars in cash you're escorting down to Colonel."

"I thought I was escorting you."

"Do I look like I need it?" she smiled. "I brought the money to the bank yesterday."

Pearse nodded his tribute to her ability to handle her business by herself. "Think you can ride all the way back if it doesn't look right?"

"Of course."

"Of course," he echoed. "I should have known."

And then the first stage pulled in with a clatter of hooves on the baked earth, a rattle of chains, and a smart popping of the whip by the driver. It was all for show, of course. It let folks know that here was a man of importance, a man who could be

22

depended upon to keep to his schedule and bring his passengers safely in.

This stage had luggage piled on the roof, and it carried a shotgun rider to boot. It could be the bullion stage, with the strongbox or boxes in the boot. Pearse sauntered over to the right wheel and pretended to examine the steel tire of the back wheel, and suddenly the shotgun rider was beside him. "Looking for something, friend?"

"Just curious."

"So was the cat," he chuckled. "It don't pay to get too curious."

"You got that right, friend," Pearse said, and he walked back to Mary Lou.

"Is this the one with the money?" she asked.

"I don't think so. It's all for show. The next one's the tickler."

"Do we ride it?"

Pearse made up his mind. "No. We get you a horse and ride a safe distance behind. If you get tired, you can always ride inside, if it's safe."

"No, thanks. We'll stick together."

"I don't like the look of this," Pearse said. "If the man I saw this morning hadn't been there, I'd feel a lot better about riding a stage, but he was and I don't."

She stirred the dust with the toe of her boot. "You could be right. On the other hand, there's safety in numbers. We ride the stage, and there's enough guns to fight."

"They wouldn't do us much good, because the others won't be ready to fight over money. It's a damn fool who does, generally, but this here is a different situation."

"Whatever you say, Charlie Pearse."

"Fine. You stay here and act like somebody waiting for the next stage. I'll go get a horse and tack for you, and then we'll figure out where to go from there."

Boom towns bred boom prices. Pearse paid a hundred and fifty dollars for a fair horse and a beat-up saddle. The horse was plug-ugly, but the legs were good and the chest was deep and it wasn't spavined or anything.

Pearse saddled the dun and his new horse for Mary Lou, and then he rode back to the stage station. He still had his doubts about the lady, but for now there was nothing to do but play out his hand the way it was dealt.

Back at the hotel where Pearse had found his lady, the clerk wriggled on his stool and told himself that it was only five hours to supper and the rest of the night off. It was not an interesting job, usually, but he got his room free and five dollars a week to boot. Even his meals were paid for. It was a lot better than digging in the mines for wages.

Of course interesting things did happen once in a while. A good-looking young woman had come in on the stage from Pierre yesterday. That was kind of interesting, trying to figure out what a young woman like that was doing in a town like Deadwood. She had told him that she was expecting someone to meet her.

That was when things started to get interesting. A tall jasper in good clothes came asking for another lady, and he was glad when the clerk told him she had already arrived. That made two ladies waiting to meet somebody.

But the best part of it was when the other fellow came in this morning and asked for the first young lady. He was carrying a saddle bag. The clerk was having an early sandwich in the little room behind the counter, but he took care of the young fellow.

After a while, the young fellow came back down the stairs and went away. Then he came back and took the other fellow's wife down the stairs. He was still carrying the saddle-bag, and she was carrying the carpetbag she'd come in with. The clerk bet that her husband was going to be awful mad when he found out his wife had run off with another man.

He squirmed over that one for a while, and then the first young woman came down the stairs. She looked disheveled, like she'd gone a round with a tame bear, and her hands were scratched, as if she'd tried to tear down a door with no tools.

"Did anyone come asking for me?" she demanded. "For Miss Mary Lou Reilly?"

"I sent him to your room," the clerk said.

"I've got to find him."

Things were heating up too fast for the clerk to keep track, and he blurted out the first thing that came to mind. "He left about half an hour ago with another lady."

"Oh, my God!"

"Looked to me like they were fixing to take the stage out of town," the clerk said.

The young woman stalked to the door without a word, and a minute later she was making tracks toward the bank, which was in the other direction from the stage station.

It wasn't an interesting job except sometimes, and then it got more interesting than a fellow could handle. Something had gone wrong here, and he didn't know what. On the other hand, he really didn't want to know. If he knew, there was a good chance he'd get in trouble. If, for example, the tall jasper who said he was married to the lady the young fellow had walked out with decided to blame the clerk for what had happened.

The clerk didn't want that at all.

Chapter Four

When Pearse returned, there was no sign of Mary Lou Reilly. He went around to the back and tied up the two horses. The stage wasn't due for half an hour, and it might well be late. The first stage had loaded and was pulling away. But there was plenty of time for them to catch the second stage, if only he could find Miss Reilly.

He was a little worried about her, truth to tell.

He needn't have been. Just when he turned the corner, she came around headed for the back. She wasn't alone. The man who'd boarded the stage and who'd been interested in Pearse's banking business was with her, and they were both smiling like a couple of people who were sharing a joke.

"Glad to meet you, Mr. Pearse," the man said. "Miss Reilly has told me a great deal about you and your responsibility. I felt it only fair to relieve you of some of it."

There was an old rule that said you didn't draw against a man who has a gun on you, and Pearse remembered it now, because the lean man in dark clothes had a lethal-looking derringer pointed at his midriff. At six feet, he couldn't miss.

"Looks like you're dealing the hand, friend," Pearse said.

He was smart enough to stay far enough back so Pearse couldn't get his own gun out or jump him, either one. There was nothing to do but what the lean man said.

"I'll take that little black bag they gave you at the bank. And then I'll escort Miss Reilly and the bag to where they're supposed to go."

"Turn it over, Charlie," the woman said. "If he isn't enough, take a look at this." She showed Pearse a Navy Colt with a cutdown barrel.

"Nothing like a pair of aces," Pearse said. He went to the saddle bag on the nigh side of his gelding and brought out the black bag.

"Where's the key?" Mary Lou Reilly asked. "The one to that padlock?"

"Banker said he was sending it on to Colonel," Pearse lied. "Guess the man didn't trust me."

"Friend, don't take offense, but you're a hell of a poor excuse for a bodyguard," the lean man said. He shifted the derringer to his left hand and stepped in close. Then he hit Pearse as hard as he could in the midriff.

Pearse had seen it coming and he braced himself, but it hurt anyway. He doubled over and went down, gasping for breath. Like Kenyon in Martin's saloon that night he'd taken Kenyon out, he knew he was going to be sore and sick. He was sick; the sore would come later.

When he heard the scuff of boots die away, he got to his knees. He hoped they hadn't taken his horses, and for a change luck was running his way. They hadn't.

They had their own, which he couldn't see, and a moment later he heard the sound of horses galloping up the street.

He got his breath back, and then he made his painful way around to the agent's office.

"A man and a woman rode out of here just now. What were they riding?"

"I figured there might be something wrong when that other jasper showed up," the agent smirked. "Yes sir. She was on a bay gelding, and he was on a gray."

"Sure about that?" Pearse asked.

"Positive," the man said, and then Pearse knew that he was lying. Deadwood hadn't changed a damn bit, he thought bitterly.

"Thank you kindly," Pearse said, and he went out in the street and looked for tracks. They were the freshest ones; no dust had settled to blur them. There was nothing outstanding about them. One horse carrying light had new calks on the offside rear hoof, the other had worn shoes all around. It was a safe bet they'd both be reshod the first chance the tall man got.

The thing that bothered Pearse the most was having to ride back to Julesburg and tell Colonel that his lady friend was a thief, and that she'd double-crossed him. The Colonel was of an age where he'd take that hard. Pearse had seen it happen too often.

On the good side, he still had the money, and until they cut open the black bag with a sharp knife, he was safe.

Pearse made a guess that they'd ridden north. The sound told him that, and he guessed too that they'd go to the hotel to the room and check out the bag in privacy. They would find the newspaper, and then they'd come looking. They'd probably head back to the stage depot to see if he was still there, and then they'd head south toward Cheyenne to catch him on the road.

They had seen his horses, and that was bad enough. Worse, he didn't have time to do any horse trading. The only thing to do was head east, maybe for Lead or Rapid City.

But they'd expect that, if they didn't catch up with him at the depot. Ride north, then. Ride right past the hotel and hope he didn't find them coming out. And then he could take up a position where he could watch their comings and goings.

Before he mounted, he pulled the Starr out of the holster and checked the cylinder. Sure enough, it was empty. He reached in his saddle bag and got out a box of shells. When he had finished reloading, he checked the Winchester as well. They hadn't bothered with that.

Pearse swung into the saddle and rode off, leading the dun he'd ridden and riding the ugly roan mare. The mare would be fresher, and it made good sense to have two horses to ride. If he were chased, he'd have the advantage of a fresh mount.

He passed the hotel without incident and rode into an alley back of a saloon. When he got the horses turned around, he waited. There were no horses tied to the hitching rail in front of the hotel; maybe they were tied up in back. He gave himself fifteen minutes. If they hadn't shown up by then, they probably had headed north out of town before opening the bag. Until they discovered the deception, they would try to put as much distance between themselves and Pearse as they could.

He waited until his allotted time was up, and then he rode south, staying off the main drag until he was safely past the edge of town.

The money was his main problem. If he went to the bank and redeposited it, he wouldn't be fulfilling his part of the bargain. If he kept it with him and tried to reach Julesburg and turn it over to Colonel, there was a good chance he'd lose it and his life to boot. Of course the pair might be mad enough when they found out he didn't have the money to kill him anyhow. He could identify them, and that would be reason enough. He wondered why they hadn't killed him back of the stage depot. Maybe they didn't want to take the time and risk somebody coming in back to investigate.

The only sure way out of the difficulty was to make time. He stayed east of the stage road, just in case the two had ridden south, and he stayed east until he'd put ten miles between him and Deadwood. At Rapid City, he joined the stage road into town. At the depot, he found that the first stage had come and gone. The second stage was due in thirty minutes. Unless there was bullion on a stage, the pickings would be slim, and Pearse didn't think his friends from Deadwood would bother holding up a stage, especially since they had an easy chance of picking up twenty thousand dollars from good old gullible Charlie Pearse. Unless, of course, they had friends and pack horses to carry the bullion. Gold was heavy.

Pearse tied his horses to the hitching rail and waited for the stage to come in. If he could tie the horses in back and ride in the coach, he'd be a little more comfortable. On the other hand, if anything happened to the stage, he'd be in the middle of it, and there would go Colonel's money.

A cloud of dust came down the street and the stage rumbled into the station. The driver and two guards stayed on the box until the team was unhitched and the fresh team led out, and then one of them went inside and came out with two tin cups of coffee. Then the driver got down and went inside. Neither of the guards went more than twenty feet from the coach. If they were putting on an act, it was a good one.

Pearse unstrapped the saddle bag with the money and went inside. There were only three passengers, and they were sitting at a deal table. There was a shabby man in a gray suit that bore testimony to his recent meals, a miner in rough work clothes, and a young woman with an air of sadness about her. She had fair hair, almost the color of ripe wheat, and she was the only one of the three who wasn't eating.

Pearse ordered a meal and sat down across from the men. "Howdy," he said. "You folks going to Laramie?"

The shabby man said he was, that he hoped to find some action there. What sort, he didn't say. The miner said he was through with mining around Deadwood; Cripple Creek might turn out better. Pearse didn't bother telling him that one boom town was much the same as any other. There were sharks and little fishes in all of them.

Both men were armed with pistols and Winchesters, and for the first time Pearse had his doubts about what the stage carried. It was possible that this was the one with the bullion, and that the two men were extra guards. But the young woman?

Maybe she was window dressing to make it look good. But no man worth his salt would put a woman in a position of risk. Not unless a good deal of money was involved. Pearse had no illusions about the ethics of human beings where money was concerned. But this young woman didn't seem to fit the mould.

"And you, miss? You headed for Cheyenne too?"

"Julesburg," she said. "I was supposed to meet someone in Deadwood, but I think he went off with the wrong person."

"That happens," Pearse said carefully. "I was sent up to Deadwood to meet somebody, but she turned out to be the wrong person after all."

The young woman was interested. "You wouldn't say who sent you, I suppose."

"A fellow they call Colonel. And you might be Mary Lou?"

She gave an audible gasp. "You're the man who sent the telegram. 'Help on way.'"

"That's me, Charlie Pearse. What happened to John Logan? You said in your telegram that he was dead."

"I don't know, Charlie. He went out of the hotel the night we arrived, and then the hotel clerk said he'd been shot in a saloon fight. It wasn't like John at all."

"You sure he's dead?"

She nodded. "I went to the undertaker's and saw him laid out. He was a friend of Colonel's, but I knew him too, and he wasn't the kind of fellow who'd get in a fight."

The two men listened politely, without interest. They had more important things to think about, Pearse guessed. Like holding up a stage.

The young woman produced a letter, well-worn and frayed around the edges. "Colonel sent this to me. That's so you'll know I'm who I say I am."

Pearse examined it briefly, handed it back. "Looks good to me. So you got as far as the hotel, and then Logan went out and got himself killed."

"I think it was an accident, Charlie. I asked in the saloon, and the bartender said two other men were fighting and there was a stray shot that caught John."

"And then what happened?"

"I went to the undertaker, and then I sent the wire to Colonel. I'd already put the thing I was supposed to deliver to Colonel in a safe place."

The two men got up and walked out, leaving Pearse and the young woman alone.

"I know about that," Pearse said.

She nodded. "Well, then I went back to the hotel to wait. When I got hungry, I went to the cafe next the hotel and got some supper, and then I went back to wait for Colonel to reply to my telegram. The clerk knocked and slipped it under the door, and then I went to sleep.

"Well, the next morning—that was yesterday—somebody knocked on my door, and I thought it was the help I'd asked for. Only it wasn't. It was a woman with a gun. She took all my spare clothes and my money, and she locked me in."

Mary Lou Reilly described the red-haired woman, right down to the riding dress and the cut-down Colt. "I've seen her before," she said. "She's a bad one."

"That's the one," Pearse said. "She and her gentleman friend held me up back at the station in Deadwood."

"And they took what you were bringing Colonel?"

Her eyes begged for a denial, but Pearse wasn't about to tell the world about the twenty thousand dollars beside his right leg. "There wasn't a lot I could do about it," he said. He thought of something else. "How did you get on the stage with no money?"

She blushed. "I went to the agent and begged, and then he said a lady had left her ticket for me. I guess that was nice of her. Otherwise I wouldn't have had a way to leave Deadwood."

"But the ticket's only good to Cheyenne, isn't it?"

"Yes. I don't know what I'm going to do when I get there."

Pearse smiled. "You've got nothing to worry about. I'm here now. I'll see to it you get to Julesburg and Colonel in one piece."

She nodded happily. "It looks like I've got through my troubles, Charlie Pearse. Thanks to you."

The two passengers had gone out a short time before. Pearse saw them talking to the driver. Something was not as it should be, he thought. He couldn't put a finger on it, but his earlier suspicion that all was not as it might be came back.

"Wait here a minute," he told Mary Lou. "I want to talk to the driver."

The two passengers boarded the stage. The driver stopped talking to the guard and came over to Pearse. "There's been a little change in plan," he said. "Another coach is coming through in about an hour, and I'm going to let you and the lady wait for it. I can't take you any further."

Pearse looked at him. "How come?"

The guard shrugged. "They made a mistake in booking the lady on. There's other passengers up ahead for this stage. The next one has plenty of room, and it's a better coach." The driver shook his head. "I'm sorry, but that's the way it has to be. You won't regret it."

"Then I guess we'll have to wait," Pearse said, putting a good face on it. "Sure wish we didn't have to."

"It's like this," the driver said smoothly. "The passengers up ahead need to make connections with a stage out of Laramie. We're ahead of the second stage by over an hour, and if we kept you two on and made them take the second stage, they'd miss their connection."

"All right. I can see that."

The driver climbed to the box. "Board!" The driver and his shotgun riders waved, and then the stage pulled out. Pearse would have bet a month's winnings that there was bullion aboard.

Mary Lou came out in time to watch the dust settle. "What happened, Charlie?"

Pearse told her, and in the telling he realized how fishy it really was. Stage lines tried to make connections, of course, but generally they held a stage over if they had to. If there had been riders at the next stop, he and Mary Lou could have gotten off there to wait for the next stage.

She frowned. "There's something wrong there. Those men didn't act like any drivers I ever saw."

"I guess they had to lay on some unexperienced men," Pearse said. "That would account for it."

"Maybe. And suppose they weren't real stage people or passengers? Suppose they just held up the stage and took it over. If there's gold aboard, it would be easy to ship the gold to wherever they wanted to go."

"You're pretty sharp. It could be that way. And they didn't want us to know where they were going, so they turned us off the first place they could without making us suspicious."

There was a lot of truth in what she said. It explained the reluctance of the driver to talk about it until he was pressed. And like the lady said, what better way to transport a heavy shipment than by stage?

"Well," she said. "What are we going to do now? Wait for the next stage?"

Pearse remembered that Colonel had said Miss Reilly could ride. There were all sorts of good reasons for waiting for the second stage, comfort among them, but something told Pearse that Rapid City was not a safe place to be. If the pair who'd relieved him of a black bag filled with newspaper had stopped to examine it, they'd be on their way to Rapid City. With no other leads, they'd tail the stage, because anybody headed for Julesburg would probably take the stage, or at least follow the stage road to Cheyenne. You could find food and maybe even a bed at the stage stations, and it was a pretty safe route.

The Bad Lands route was rougher and riskier. The Indians were pretty much on the reservation now, but there was always the chance of running into renegades or miners on their way to or from the gold fields.

"Just considering the options," Pearse smiled. "Are you game to ride a horse all the way to Julesburg?"

She looked him over, maybe making up her mind whether or not to trust him, and then she said, "I'm game. I'll need some clothes and a horse."

"I've got the horse. We'll get you some clothes. You want to ride side saddle I guess?"

"Some pants and a shirt will do fine," she said. "I'd guess it would be safer if I looked like a boy."

"Probably would," Pearse said. "What size do you wear?"

He left her at the station with the horses, and then he walked off down the street in search of a dry-goods store.

Time was running out, but he forced himself to shop carefully. If they were going to be out for three or four days, it was important to get the right stuff.

He got boots for ten dollars, pants and shirt for another five, and then he went further down the street to a hardware store and checked out guns. He got a well-worn Colt and belt and holster for twenty-five, and the merchant obligingly threw in a box of shells.

Chapter Five

Everything that had happened so far had made Pearse extra careful, and he approached the stage station from the rear. Nobody was around, so he checked out the stock. Six well-run horses were busy with a pile of hay. They'd been wiped down, but they still showed traces of hard work. He guessed the second stage had come and gone while he was busy with his shopping.

He walked around to the front and collected Mary Lou Reilly. She said the second stage had been packed when it came in. There had been no room for even one passenger. Somehow, it didn't surprise Pearse a bit.

He handed the clothes to Mary Lou, who promptly disappeared into the privy to change, and then he bought a feed of oats for the horses. By the time she reappeared, they had been fed and watered, and he watched while she adjusted the stirrups on the mare. She knew what she was doing, he thought. Probably been around horses quite a lot in her time.

They headed out of town along the stage route until they were out of sight of town. He started looking for a good place to turn off, and eventually he found it. A party of riders had crossed the trail at one point, and Pearse turned into their tracks. The riders had headed east, and that was fine with him. With luck, they'd find another good turnoff, and then they'd be safe from whatever might come up behind them.

About two hours out, he stopped to rest the horses, and Mary Lou got curious. "Why aren't we following the stage route? You never said, you just turned off."

Pearse grinned. "Haven't you figured it out yet?"

"I'm guessing. Somehow you got the money back, and now you're trying to keep ahead of them all the way to Julesburg."

"That's about the size of it. Yes, I've got the money, and yes, I think they're going to be following us. They probably don't know about you—I'd say they figure you're on the stage with a ticket for Laramie—but they're surely after me by now."

"If they miss you, they're only going to be waiting for us in Julesburg."

"Julesburg is a long way off. We'll worry about them when we get there," Pearse said. Right now, he was worried about what they were going to eat for three days, maybe four. He'd dumped out the food to make room for the money, so there was nothing but coffee and whatever he could shoot.

"I never thought I'd be coming on horseback," she said. "I guess that's one of those experiences Colonel's always talking about."

She made a good-looking boy, Pearse decided. If you looked real close at her face, you could tell the difference, but she had a slight figure that was hidden under the flannel shirt, the bunched-in canvas pants, and the wide-brimmed hat. A good thing, too. The tall man and the lean lady would be looking for a lone rider, not two riders together. They might be looking for a young woman too, depending upon how closely they'd checked the stage depot, but they wouldn't be looking for a slight young man.

All told, Pearse was pretty pleased with himself. He foraged for a strip of jerky in one of the saddle bags and handed it to the young woman. "This is supper," he said. "Make it last. We'll have meat tomorrow, if I can risk hunting."

"I can go without a meal," Mary Lou said. "It never hurt anybody I ever knew of."

She was being a good sport about it all, and for a moment he wished she weren't going to Julesburg to marry Colonel. But that was as far as that wish got. Pearse guessed he wasn't the marrying kind, and besides Colonel had trusted him. Pearse wasn't the kind to betray a man's trust.

He climbed a little hill and stopped to look west toward the stage route. Off in the distance there was a cloud of dust, faint as fog on a spring morning. He took out his field glasses and checked it more closely. At least three riders, as near as he could make out, and headed in their direction. They might be harmless, but Pearse didn't care to find out.

"Looking at that dust behind us?" Mary Lou asked.

"Just checking it out."

"Do you think they've tracked us?"

No fear, no panic. Only honest curiosity. Pearse approved. "I don't think so. I don't see how they could have made up so much time so fast. But it might be better if we made tracks."

She got up and swung into the saddle while Pearse was still strapping the saddle bag. "What are we waiting for?" she smiled.

A couple of miles further on, the tracks of the other horses led them to a small creek. The riders who had been before them had watered there. So did Pearse. But the other riders had gone on across. Pearse led the way upstream. "We'll follow the water for awhile," he said. "If we're lucky, they won't notice that we left the trail."

It was a nice shallow stream, sometimes narrowing to a trickle, sometimes widening out to pools. Willows lined the banks, and he even found a good place to leave the stream where there were large pebbles that wouldn't take prints.

They rode behind a little hill and he explained to Mary Lou where they were and where they had to go. "We're going to hit the Bad Lands tomorrow, and then we're going to head south for the Pine Ridge Indian reservation. We ought to be able to buy some flour and bacon there, maybe even a meal if the agent is happy with us. After that, we cut straight south to Julesburg."

"Can we get water?"

"This side of the Bad Lands, yes. Once we're in them, no. We'll have to ride maybe thirty or forty miles without. But we can get water near Pine Ridge."

Pearse left her to climb the hill and scout the route. When he got near the top, he went down on all fours and crawled the rest of the way. The detour they'd taken to go up the creek had slowed them down, and he could see the riders. There were four, not three, and they were leading two pack-mules. Pearse was happy to see that they weren't the pair who'd held him up, and then he looked closer.

The driver and the shotgun and the two passengers of the first stage were the riders. It didn't take a real smart man to figure that those pack-mules were toting bullion.

He watched them while they passed within three hundred yards of the hill, and then he watched them while they turned generally southeast. Just about where Pearse wanted to go.

"I'd rather have them ahead of us than behind us," Mary Lou said when Pearse told her. "Even if they'll be watching their back trail, they won't be chasing us."

"I wonder how they did it. Took a stage, I guess, and ran it the way it was supposed to go, and didn't leave a trace of the real driver or the real passengers."

She shuddered. "I don't think I want to know. I'm just glad they kicked us off and didn't take us with them."

"We'd be a meal for the coyotes by now," Pearse agreed. "Maybe we'll get real lucky and your namesake and her partner will run into them. It would surely be a thieves' get-together."

If he didn't want to run into them somewhere along the trail, Pearse was going to have to strike off in a different direction. Again, it was a case of making haste slowly. He climbed the hill again and watched the dust they raised until he had a fair idea of where they were headed. It looked to him like they were headed for the Bad Lands, and that made sense. If they wanted to make themselves scarce, it was a good choice.

Erosion had created the Bad Lands, cutting the original flat land into buttes and gullies, and it was a good tracker who could find his way through them without getting lost.

If the four outlaws had friends waiting there with fresh horses, they could easily outdistance any pursuit. If they didn't, they could lie low for a week or so, coming out only for water, and by that time the posse would have given up. Pearse had a good idea how these things worked. He'd ridden with posses a time or two.

When the dust settled into the distance and he couldn't see any further than a mile, he went back to where he had left Mary Lou with the horses.

"Looks like they're headed for the Bad Lands themselves," Pearse told her. "We'll have to stay clear of them. We'll camp here for the night, and in the morning we can strike out for Pine Ridge."

"Fine with me," Mary Lou said, and she began to unroll the blankets and settled herself in a little hollow. Pearse took the remaining blanket and rolled himself in it. It would be cold sleeping tonight. But he'd slept cold before.

As he went to sleep, he thought that there were very few young women who could have accepted the situation the way she had. Colonel was a very lucky man.

Mary Lou Reilly awakened just before dawn to the feel of mist on her face. Now would be a good time for kicking a fire back into life and making coffee, she thought. But it was a dry camp, no fire and no water. Just the way I would have done it if I'd been alone, she thought. Colonel picked a smart man.

She liked what she had seen of Charlie Pearse. He could think on his feet—the way he'd hidden the money from the pair of thieves had proved that—and he wasn't afraid to tackle what had turned into a very difficult assignment. He was also a gentleman. He was friendly without being forward, and he didn't try to boss her the way some men would have. He simply took charge, the way Colonel would have done. Colonel never threw his weight around either. He didn't have to.

Back in the old days, when Colonel had been a sergeant, he had been noted for his even temper dealing with recruits. He acted like a schoolmaster, making sure they learned what they were supposed to, taking care of their needs ahead of his own. He was somewhere next to God in her eyes, and it was somewhat of a surprise to find that he was interested in her too.

Charlie Pearse woke up and shook himself, for all the world like a dog getting ready to go chase down a rabbit for breakfast.

"Good morning," she said. "Ready for the day?"

"Just about," he grinned. "You sleep all right?"

"Just fine. Where are we going today?"

He shook his head from side to side. "Can't say, as yet. Just head south and hope for the best. I don't think we've been followed so far."

It would be hard for him, she thought. A flatlander coming into hills always had a problem. He couldn't see over the next hill, he couldn't know what was there, and he tended to spook at nothing at all. And that could lead him to rush ahead whenever he saw a flat piece of ground where he felt at home. And that could lead him straight into trouble.

So far, Charlie Pearse had shown none of those symptoms. He knew hills about as well as he knew flatland, and he went forward without hesitation, once he had scouted the land to his front. She felt safe with him.

They went from one hill to another, and eventually the land got a little smoother, a little flatter. He was careful to check their backtrail as well as look ahead, but she could tell he was still leery of the country. There was no space to see ahead, no place to hide if somebody was watching from one of the hills.

When the sun was almost overhead, Pearse picked a spot to rest. It was just over the crest of a hill dotted with pines. He could see to the front, and if he climbed six feet, he could see to the rear as well. Mary Lou looked also. There was nothing moving anywhere in the land, and she guessed it would be safe enough to look for something to shoot. About all he was apt to get was sage hen, which made mighty good eating. And then she saw their dinner.

"Can we have a fire, Charlie?"

"A little one. Enough to make coffee."

"I see dinner waiting."

"Where?"

She pointed to one of the pines. "There's a couple of squirrels playing around up there."

"I was thinking about them. Figure they're big enough to make a meal, go ahead and shoot them."

She pulled the Colt from the holster in one fluid motion, bringing her left hand up to cover her right, and she took the head off the first squirrel with her first shot. The second squirrel danced around looking for his mate, and then he paused to look down and she shot it too.

"Mighty fine shooting," Pearse said. "You didn't spoil any meat. Where'd you learn to shoot like that?"

"Colonel taught me whatever my father didn't. They were both pretty good."

"That's not the Army way," Pearse said. "They use one hand and they stand flat to the target."

She smiled. "My father and Colonel didn't do everything the Army way."

Pearse got out his hunting knife and dressed the squirrels, taking the hides off in one easy shucking motion. Then he laid the carcasses on a pine twig while Mary Lou built a small fire of twigs and pine cones. A thin thread of smoke rose in the still air, but it couldn't be seen at any distance, she thought.

Chapter Six

Pearse lit a cigar with a twig from the fire. The squirrels were roasting nicely. He and Mary Lou had run branches through them, and they turned them occasionally. It wouldn't take long, he thought; they were pretty small squirrels.

Pearse was impressed with Mary Lou's shooting. He might have guessed that Colonel hadn't pulled his lady out of a hat. Obviously, they had known each other well, and they were preparing to get hitched on the basis of past acquaintance. That was a whole lot better than getting hitched without knowing anything about the person you were marrying. Pearse could see that this was the kind of woman Colonel would pick: somebody capable and tough without losing any of her womanliness.

When the squirrels were about done, Pearse laid his on a flat rock and went to his saddle bags for a couple of pieces of hardtack. That was dinner. He got rid of his squirrel in about five good bites, but nothing ever tasted half so good.

When the meal was finished, he stamped a small hole in the ground big enough to get rid of the fur and the bones and the entrails, and then they were on their way again.

They rode all through the hot afternoon, and once they came to a small creek where they could fill the canteens and water the horses. Pearse checked the banks carefully and couldn't find a trace of footprints. So far, so good. It was a big country, and it looked as if it had swallowed the four men and their pack animals, although for all he knew they could be over the next hill.

Dusk came late, and about time for it to get dark Pearse found an antelope and downed it with the Winchester. There was no other way to do it; he risked the noise of the shot and hoped luck was running with them. He wondered where the bogus Miss Reilly and her friend had got to; he hoped they had followed the stage road, but there was no way of telling.

Before it got too dark to see, he climbed a rise, leaving the horses with Mary Lou. A long way off to the left he saw a pinpoint of light that might have been a fire made by the four men they'd seen earlier. It was a big enough fire, he guessed, but it was too far for him to make out anything, even with the field-glasses.

Mary Lou found a hollow where they could build a small fire without advertising it to the whole country, and Pearse butchered the antelope. It was a small one, even for a pronghorn, but he got some good steaks out of it, and he broiled a couple for supper and charred another four to take with them.

He was pretty happy about the whole thing, sitting there at the fire across from Mary Lou, munching away at fresh meat. He took credit for fooling the opposition, which was what good poker was all about, and he came close to breaking his arm reaching over to pat himself on the back.

And then he heard it. Horses, maybe six or more, not too far off. Close enough for the riders to smell the smoke from the fire, even if they could only see the glow.

"We're getting company," Pearse said quietly. "Get off to the side and get behind a tree."

The horses stopped as Mary Lou scrambled to the cover of a rock ledge off to the side. In a moment she was gone, vanished into the blackness beyond the fire, and Pearse eased out his Winchester and waited.

"Hello the fire," a man said. Pearse looked up and pretended to be surprised. "All right to come in?"

"Come ahead and welcome."

It was kind of unnecessary, Pearse thought, because the man had already come close. He was medium-sized, no bigger than

Pearse, and he looked to be about forty or so, with a heavy drooping mustache. He wore a gun, but he wasn't making any moves toward it.

"Where's your friend?"

"Around."

The man flipped back his coat and showed Pearse a star. "Clinton, U. S. Marshal. I need to talk to you and your friend a minute. Want to call him in?"

"Mary Lou? Come on in. It's all right."

She got out from behind her tree and walked over to the fire slowly. She had the Colt in its holster, but she was ready.

"All right, boys," the Marshal called out. "Come on in and set. We'll take us a little breather."

He had followed them without too much trouble, knowing something of their story. Pearse was surprised. "It made good sense to leave the stage trail and head east," he said. "Seeing as how you were headed for Julesburg anyway. I talked to the stage agent at Rapid City, and he told me you and the lady had figured to take the stage, and then the driver wouldn't take you and said to wait for the second stage."

"Shoot," Pearse said. "And all along I thought I was being smart."

Clinton grinned. The riders with him had dismounted and were grazing their horses. Two of them stayed close to Pearse's and Mary Lou's horses, just in case.

"You were pretty smart, all things considered. You rode the stage out of Deadwood. Who was with you?"

Mary Lou described the driver and the shabby man who was looking for a new town. Pearse confirmed, adding a detail or two she had overlooked.

"That kind of checks out. Now why did you go chasing around all over the place? It cost me some time, but I had to go slow so I wouldn't miss anything."

Mary Lou cut in and told him about the woman who had taken her money and clothes at gunpoint. She didn't mention the money Pearse was carrying.

"Charlie here was bringing me to Julesburg. He had promised Colonel Reynolds, and he was bringing him something he'd left behind up in Deadwood."

Pearse wished she hadn't said that, because it put him in the position of saying what it was he was bringing, but there was no help for it. It had been said, and that was that.

"And this man and woman came along and took what you had to deliver. Is that it?" Clinton asked.

"That's about the way it was." Pearse said.

"'About' is right," Clinton smiled. "The reason you were running off and leaving the stage trail is because you made a switch, and you knew when they caught up with you, they'd take the real goods."

Pearse nodded.

Mary Lou had been busy with the fire. "Anybody wants coffee, there's a fresh pot. Just help yourselves."

The men of the posse fished for cups and came closer to hear what there was to hear.

"I ain't going to ask you what it was you were supposed to deliver," Clinton said. "Seeing as how it's personal and none of my business."

Pearse nodded. "If you have to know, I can tell you, but I'd rather not, seeing it's Colonel's business and none of mine."

"Fair enough. Now the people on that stage the lady rode took the stage from its rightful driver before Deadwood. They didn't hurt anybody, but they tied up the driver and the guard and the three passengers and left them out in the hay barn behind the Deadwood depot. It was kind of embarassing, because that stage had about sixty thousand dollars worth of gold aboard. They were smart enough to pretend they were the regular people for the stage, and they took you on at Deadwood to make it look good. You were the icing on the cake. But when they got to Rapid City, they didn't need you any more, so they bumped you off."

"We can count ourselves lucky, I guess," Pearse said. "If we'd insisted, they would have had to get rid of us down the line."

Clinton nodded. "They might have just tied you up so the second stage could pick you up. On the other hand, they might not have wanted to leave witnesses."

"They'd have shot us, more than likely," Mary Lou said.

The Marshal got a stub pipe out of his pocket and stuffed it with shag. "More'n likely," he said. "Like the gent said, you two were lucky. What interests me—and probably does you—is how the man and the woman who took the lady prisoner and relieved her of her money and her clothes knew that you'd be there. Knew what you were going to do, and even knew that Mr. Pearse here was going to show up to escort you to Deadwood?"

"I don't know," Mary Lou said. "I didn't even know who was coming to fetch me."

"There's one thing," Pearse said. "Colonel owns a livery stable, and he said something about one of his men overhearing a man say something about a big gold shipment."

"That doesn't explain how they knew you were coming," Clinton remarked.

"If somebody talked about the gold shipment, they could have found out about my coming. If one of the men knew I'd left town, word could have gotten out."

"I suppose so," Clinton said. "And the lady could have been followed on the other end." He puffed at his pipe until the coal glowed. "Right now I'm looking for the men who took that stage. We heard about it just after the second stage left Julesburg, but by the time we got to Rapid City the first stage had pulled out. My guess would be they had somebody waiting for them with horses, and they ditched the stage off the trail. Maybe even left the team hitched up so they'd have more of a start."

"Where'd you find the stage?" Mary Lou asked.

"Figured that out, did you?" Clinton smiled. "It was about a mile west of the trail, in a little canyon. Them big wheels leave tracks in a dry summer, so it wasn't too hard. It wasn't too hard to figure that they'd be headed east, either. They're just medium smart."

"You tracked them?" Pearse asked.

"Yep. They went west for a little, and then they cut east on a rocky place where they figured their tracks would be hid, but we circled until we found them, and we followed them right up until we smelled wood smoke from your fire." He knocked his pipe out on the heel of his boot. "Now what have you got to tell me?"

Pearse grinned. "I saw them. About mid-afternoon yesterday they were headed this way. There were four of them, the same four who'd been on the stage. They were headed southeast, the way we wanted to go, and they had two pack mules."

"Any more?"

"About an hour ago I shot an antelope and I looked around before I made a fire. About four miles from here I saw another fire. I looked through my field glasses, but I couldn't see a thing. It might have been a decoy fire, but I don't think so. I think it was the way some amateurs do, run like hell, plan everything out, and then make a stupid mistake like lighting a fire."

Clinton nodded. "The driver used to work for Russell and Majors, and they laid him off when business got bad. The man with him on the box would have been Pete Hawes. He's a hired gun. The other two, I don't know. Probably a couple of fellows out of work and looking for some easy money on the owl-hoot trail. Show me where that fire was."

Pearse climbed the little hill with Clinton. There was no sign of a fire now, not even a glow, but Pearse remembered that the fire had been in line with a hill taller than the rest, and he showed it to Clinton.

"Figures," he said. "They might could be headed for the Bad Lands, but I don't think so. They're going to want to get some-wheres close to Denver, where they can trade in that gold for silver dollars, a little at a time." He looked at Pearse. "I hate to do this to you, Charlie, but I'm going to ask you and the lady to come with us. We can always use another man, and I need you two to help identify them."

"As long as we get to Julesburg," Charlie Pearse said. "I'll talk to the lady."

"You got five minutes," Clinton said, and then they went down the hill and joined the others.

Chapter Seven

Clinton was not unhappy with the way things had turned out. Four of his men had been anxious to return to Deadwood, and it was a stroke of fortune that he'd found two riders to replace them. The young woman wouldn't be much use, he guessed, but she could at least identify the men she'd ridden the stage with, and Pearse looked like the kind of man you could count on.

The Marshal was not too happy with the men he was chasing; none of them was especially smart. None of them had had the brains to plan to take over a stage, and that indicated the presence of another man. Who he was remained to be seen, but Clinton didn't rule out the possibility that he was the man who had been with the lady who had relieved Pearse of his burden. Pearse had sensed something and out-smarted them, but that still didn't mean that the man Pearse had described had lacked the brains for taking the stage over.

The two men Clinton kept were Tom Henry and Alois Krause. Henry was a self-contained man, not given to showing emotion. Some might call him cold. He was small in appearance, but he had broad shoulders and a toughness about him that kept him going when the going got rough. Krause was first-generation American, and like many of his kind, he was eager to be accepted. He did everything with precision, he was happy to follow Clinton's orders, and he showed initiative in making suggestions. He also had a natural ability in tracking. Clinton guessed that he had been a soldier at one time, either here or in Germany.

Pearse explained to Mary Lou what Clinton wanted. She was in favor of going along with the posse. "We're stuck out here on our own," she said. "If we've got them with us, we're in pretty fair shape to get to Julesburg in one piece. Now that Clinton knows about the two who tried to get Colonel's money in Deadwood we've got a lot of help in case they catch up with us."

Pearse chuckled. "Another thing you didn't mention is that we've got no choice in the matter. In case you don't remember, Clinton's a U. S. Marshal, and he can ask us to go with him any time he wants."

She gave him a wry look. "I got a good memory, Charlie. I know what the score is."

The four riders Clinton had picked to return mounted up and headed back the way they'd come. "We'll take another ten minutes or so," Clinton said, "and then we'll take a look around where that fire was."

Pearse guessed Clinton was shooting in the dark, hoping that the fire belonged to the men he was chasing, and taking a short cut so he wouldn't have to go back to where he'd lost the trail he'd been following before. That was probably why Clinton had followed their tracks to the fire instead of trying to follow the tracks of the men he was chasing.

The night had turned cool, and it was a welcome respite from the heat of the day, but along toward midnight it got cold. Krause sniffed around ahead of the rest trying to pick up tracks, and finally he succeeded. He called a halt while Clinton dismounted and examined them, and finally they decided that they were the same tracks, right down to the pack animals.

"How long ago?" Clinton asked.

Krause shoved his hat back on his head and thought about it. "Maybe five, six hours. But they've got to have stopped for the night."

"Maybe. Could be they'll just push on."

"They got tired horses," Henry said. "They don't stop, they'll kill a horse, and then they'll have real problems."

"So will we," Pearse cut in.

Clinton didn't pay him any mind. "We'll keep moving for a while yet."

And so they plodded on while the night grew old and the sliver of moon went down, and then it was too dark to see the tracks. Clinton called a halt, and they unsaddled and let the horses graze. Mary Lou rolled up in her blankets and was asleep as soon as she hit the ground. Pearse noted with approval that she slept on her back with the Colt on her chest under the blanket. And then he too was asleep, and the night faded into dawn.

They made a cold breakfast of pronghorn steak as soon as it was light, and then they caught up the horses and were on their way again.

The tracks led to a little rise in the ground, and there they found the ashes of the fire. There were horse droppings and an empty tobacco sack and the frayed end of a rope to mark the spot, and Clinton was happy. It was the first real evidence that the men he was hunting had been at the fire Pearse had seen.

"They were not here long," Krause said. "They maybe built them a fire and rested for an hour and then moved out."

"You sure?" Clinton asked.

"Yah, I'm sure. They didn't even cook or make coffee. No grounds, you see."

They split, casting about to find the trail out of camp, and it was hard because the riders had split up and gone off in different directions. But eventually the trails all headed west, and they came together three miles out of camp.

"What in hell are they up to?" Henry wondered. "They rode east, and now they're headed west."

"Looks to me like they're going to get back to the stage route," Clinton said. "Maybe they're going to switch horses at one of the stations. They've broken trail a couple of times, and maybe they figure it's safe."

"They're dumb enough," Henry said. "Building a fire for everybody and his neighbor to see."

Krause laughed. "Not so dumb, I think. It took us out of our way and cost us some time."

"We'll follow the trail," Clinton said. "But there's a stage station about fifteen miles west of here, and I'd bet money that's where they're headed."

They set off again, and now the sun was hot on their backs and the tired horses made heavy going of it. The hills slowed them down, nice green hills with white and yellow and orange outcroppings of rocks. The air was heavy with the smell of sage and the clean smell of pines on the hills. It was pretty country, Pearse thought, and it was a shame they were traveling too fast to enjoy it.

Clinton had called the turn, and he was right. The trail led right to the station he'd mentioned, and while he talked to the agent, the rest of them unsaddled and watered the horses. Pearse went over to Mary Lou and asked her how she was holding up.

"Just fine, Charlie. How about you?"

"Not too shabby. Looks like we're going to get to Cheyenne one way or another, doesn't it?"

She smiled. "Just as long as we get to Julesburg some time this year, I don't mind."

They all filed in and sat at the table of deal boards, and the agent's wife came out of the back with a big kettle of stew, a couple of loaves of fresh-baked bread, and a pot of coffee.

"Eat hearty," Clinton advised. "Might be the last good meal we get for a while."

The agent came over to the table, maybe to listen, but probably just to talk. Pearse could see where a man could get lonesome with nobody much to talk to between stages. Of course he had his wife and the men who hitched up the teams and cared for the stock, but after a while there would be nothing new to talk about, and the same old conversations would keep repeating themselves.

The agent was an older man, maybe in his fifties, and he had a lot of news to tell. Clinton had heard it before, Pearse guessed, but the agent was anxious to talk and Clinton was just as anxious to eat.

The four men they had been tracking had stopped here, changed horses, and allowed as how they were headed for Platte Bridge, which was a good hundred miles to the east. He described the horses they'd swapped for, and he told them about the way the shabby man had hung back waiting for the others to say something. The shabby man was low man on the totem pole, Pearse guessed. Either that, or he was the boss of the operation.

News had spread about the stage that had not only been robbed but stolen to boot, and the agent said he'd never heard of anything like it.

Clinton had a theory. "They had to find out if the stage had gold on it," he said. "Getting caught for stopping a stage ain't the end of the world. A year or so in prison, and then they're free as birds. But getting caught for stealing maybe sixty thousand dollars worth of gold nuggets is another matter."

"Money makes people do funny things," Krause said, and Pearse wondered how honest any of them would be if they knew he had twenty thousand dollars in paper inside his saddlebag. So far, only he and Mary Lou and Clinton knew about it.

They took their time eating, because it would be a long time before they stopped again. When they went outside, Clinton had used government paper to requisition spare mounts for each of them. "President Hayes can pay for them horses," Tom Henry chuckled. "Fair's fair, and I plumb wore mine out getting here."

"That was all a lot of bunk, that about Platte Bridge," Clinton said. "They're probably headed for Cheyenne, once they get away from the stage route. If we lose the trail, we'll head for Laramie, and if that don't do it, we'll head into Cheyenne."

They were riding the horses Clinton had picked up for them, and Pearse guessed that they were the same ones the outlaws had ridden in. They had had six hours rest, he figured, because the agent had said the outlaws had been there about nine in the morning. Of course the agent kept time by his watch, and everybody's watch was set a little different, but that was close enough.

They rode off into the hot afternoon, following the trail with difficulty because the gang had wisely followed the stage route so that their hoof-prints would be blurred by the prints left by the last stage. Krause told them to spread out and to let him know any time there were prints to the side of the trail. They covered maybe six miles that way, and then the tracks of six horses showed to the west of the stage route.

"Laramie or Cheyenne," Clinton said. "Take your pick."

They followed the new trail, and at the end of three hours they stopped to change horses. By the looks of the trail, the new horses the gang had gotten were beginning to tire. Pearse thought it wouldn't be long before they caught up with the outlaws. He was anxious for it to be over, but he was also concerned about Mary Lou. He didn't want to see Colonel's lady caught in the middle of a gun fight.

They came to a river, in this hot summer narrowed down to a trickle of its usual self, and they rode down to it and watered the horses. Pearse spotted the place where the outlaws had done the same and ridden across the stream to the north.

Krause spotted a thread of smoke over the next rise, and he and Clinton went ahead to investigate. Clinton came back quickly. "Let me use them glasses of yours, Charlie. I think we got them now."

Pearse went along to see. Down the slope was a small log house and a log barn and a corral. In the corral were six horses, and smoke was coming from the chimney of the house.

Dusk blurred the sharp edges of the buildings, but no light showed from the window of the house. Clinton looked at the horses for a long time. "Looks like what we been following," he said. "We'll just stop here and wait for dark, and then we'll move in and see what we got."

There was always the chance that the outlaws had swapped horses again and ridden on, but it was a chance they had to take. Pearse called softly to Clinton. "Suppose we split. I can circle around and make sure they haven't swapped horses and ridden out already."

Clinton nodded. "All right. Just stay out of sight. Two of you go out, one to the north, one to the south. When you meet up with the other fellow, hold up where you are, unless you've found new tracks. I'll give it an hour, and if you're not back by then, we'll come join you."

"What if we haven't found anything?" Mary Lou asked.

Clinton looked at her. "This is no work for a woman, miss. You stay back here."

She gave him a mischievous grin and rode off to the north. "You take the south, Charlie," she called out.

Clinton stiffened, and for a moment Pearse thought he might be having a stroke. There was nothing much he could do about it though. Mary Lou had him by the short hairs. If he rode after her or called out to her, there was a good chance somebody down at the house would hear him.

"I'll take the south," Pearse told him. "Don't worry about Mary Lou. She knows country and she can track. She's pretty good with a sixgun, too."

"That's nice to know," Clinton said sarcastically. "All right, go ahead. Don't forget what I told you though. Wait up for us unless you don't find tracks. If there's nothing out there and you figure they're inside the house, send her back to let us know. I want the house circled so we can take them."

Pearse gave the reins of his spare horse to Krause. Henry already had Mary Lou's.

There was still light enough to see by, and Pearse found no tracks by the time he had reached the other side of the valley. He waited up for Mary Lou. She pulled up beside him a minute or two later.

"Nothing," she said. "They've got to be down there still."

"They could have split and gone out separately."

"No pack horses," she said. "Nobody was leading a horse."

"We'll wait for somebody to come around and tell us what to do," Pearse said. "I'd bet they're still in there, and they aren't going to be easy to get out. Let's see what Clinton's got up his sleeve."

They waited in the cool night while mosquitoes from the stream below came up to take bites. Pearse didn't want to risk lighting a cigar, which would have chased some of them away. Even though they were a couple of hundred yards from the nearest building, there was always the chance that somebody'd see the flame of the match or the glow of a cigar.

"I wonder what happened to the pair who tied you up," Pearse said. "I recognized the man as the one who boarded the stage the night before."

"I might know them," Mary Lou said. "I mean, they grabbed me and I didn't get a good look at them before they tied a rag over my eyes, but I have an idea."

"Who are they?"

"My father said never to accuse anybody if I wasn't sure," she said primly. "So I'm not saying."

Krause came up behind them so softly that Pearse didn't hear him until the last moment. "Thought I had you," he said. "Just checking to see how good a watch you was keeping."

"Good enough," Pearse told him. "What's going on?"

"Clinton's going to wait until full dark, and then he's going to ride in alone and see what he can find out. He said he didn't think any of the gang would recognize him."

"I hope he's right," Pearse said. "Anybody stole a whole stagecoach isn't going to think twice about shooting a plain old Marshal."

Krause rode back with their information, and they waited some more. They were already as close as they ought to be, either to help Clinton or to keep anybody from getting away. Pearse guessed that Krause and Henry would move in from the east to cover Clinton.

It was not full night when Clinton rode up to the house. He called out and got no answer, so he dismounted and knocked on the door. Pearse could hear the thuds. Clinton kicked the door open and waited. If anything was going to happen, now was the time. There might be nothing at all; on the other hand, all hell could break loose at any moment.

After what seemed like forever, a match flared, and Clinton appeared in the doorway holding a coal oil lamp. He them to come in, and they met Krause and Henry in the dooryard.

"It ain't pretty," Clinton warned. "But you might as well see what we're up against."

An old man was lying on the floor with half his head missing. Across the room a woman about the same age was huddled in a corner. She had been shot through the chest, and her dress was dark with blood. She hadn't died quickly.

Mary Lou gagged and went back to her horse. Pearse felt like doing the same.

"I'd say it happened about four hours ago," Clinton said. "They came here and probably got spare horses. I'd guess the old man objected, and they didn't want to bargain, so they shot him. When his missus came out, they shot her too."

Most killing was wholly unnecessary, Pearse thought, and this was one of those killings. The outlaws could have tied up the old folks and left them, the way they had the driver and passengers of the stage. But they didn't. They could have offered the old man money. But they didn't. They could have just let it alone and ridden off, but they didn't do that either. It was a senseless, spur-of-the-moment thing, and Pearse couldn't help but think that if there hadn't been all that money involved, two people who hadn't harmed anyone would still be alive.

"Maybe the old folks knew them by sight," Henry suggested.

"Might could be," Clinton said. "Let's look for a Bible."

"Bible?" Henry puzzled. "What do we want that for?"

"It'll have their names in it, and that'll maybe give us an idea as to why they got killed."

Krause found the Bible on a shelf in the bedroom, and like Clinton said, there were names in it. John and Mary Norton had been married for thirty years. Clinton got out his little notebook and copied the names, while Pearse and Krause went out to the barn and found a shovel and a spade. They dug a grave in the sandy soil behind the house.

Clinton rummaged through scrap until he found a flat board, and he cut the names and the date into the soft pine.

By common consent, they moved away from the house, and then they talked.

There was no indication that any of the horses had been led, and it puzzled Clinton for a long while, until Mary Lou pointed out a way. "They rode out without a lead and let the horses follow them," she said. "That way it would look like they hadn't been here at all."

"What about the old folks?" Clinton wondered. "Sooner or later somebody would have come along and found them."

"Not everybody would walk into a house when nobody answered the the knock," she pointed out. "It could have been weeks."

Henry grunted approval. "Lady's right. Remember, they hadn't figured us to be this close behind them. For all they know, we're still over east, maybe in the Bad Lands."

"That could be," Clinton agreed. "If that's so, they're apt to be careless. Let's just make sure we aren't. They're desperate men, and they're going to shoot on sight. When we catch up with them, we're going to try to take them alive, but I don't want anybody here getting hurt. If you see one bad move, shoot for keeps."

They waited, huddled under blankets to keep off the mosquitoes, until the quarter moon came up, and then they set out in a fan-shaped pattern to find the tracks of the killers. It took the better part of an hour before the separate trails came together again.

For maybe another hour they followed the trail, and then Krause saw what might have been a fire ahead. The rest of them followed him until they could smell the wood smoke, and then they saw the fire. It was on low ground, down in a draw near the stream that passed near the house. "I'll take Tom Henry with me," Clinton directed. "Me and Tom'll get around to the west and box them in on that side. Krause, work your way up to that little hill on the south and cover the camp. Pearse, you and the lady cover the east. I'm going to walk in and brace them."

"Everybody better get in close," Tom Henry advised. "We don't want to go shooting each other."

Pearse and Mary Lou crept forward until they could see the faint glow of the low fire and four sets of blankets rolled up near it. Four horses were tied to a picket line stretched between two trees. They were still saddled.

Clinton called out, and after a minute or so Krause whistled from his hill. The trap was set; all they had to do was wake up and find themselves in a cross-fire if they made a wrong move.

But nothing happened.

"Hold the horses," Pearse told Mary Lou. "Whatever happens, don't let go of them."

He picked a target and sighted on it. Clinton came into the camp area, gun drawn, and kicked at one of the blankets. It fell open and the man inside rolled over limply and lay still. Clinton cursed and walked over to the next blanket and kicked it. The same thing happened.

Pearse rested the Winchester against his hip and came down the hill. Henry and Krause came in the same way, guns in hand.

Clinton looked pale in the glow of the dying fire. "Dead. Every one of them dead."

It wasn't too hard to figure out what had happened, Pearse thought. The four had decided to make camp, sure that they had eluded pursuit. They had concentrated on making a fire and cooking their supper. Their weapons were leaning against rocks, and two of them had even taken off their gun belts. One or two men on the far side of the little stream had picked them off while they scrambled for their guns, but nobody had gotten that far.

"That was in cold blood," Krause said. "You can see how it happened. He shot them from across the little river there, maybe with a good repeating rifle. They had no chance to fight."

"Damned if I can feel sorry for a one of them," Clinton growled. "After what they did back there at the house, they only got what was coming to them."

"Bury them?" Henry asked.

"Hell, no. We lost too much time already." Clinton said. "Let's be looking around for tracks."

They hunted until they found what they were looking for. The sharpshooter had taken the pack animals, each carrying a hundred pounds in gold, and he'd taken the best of the horses, Pearse guessed.

Mary Lou nudged him. "There were two of them," she said. Two guns, two people."

"Two men?"

"One's riding light," she said, and then she trotted off to catch up with Clinton.

Pearse gave Clinton credit. He listened carefully to Mary Lou, and then he got down and examined the tracks. When he remounted, he gave the rest his opinion. "Like the lady says, there was two of them. One's riding light, and it could be it's the same woman who held up Miss Reilly here."

Krause nodded agreement. "It could be a woman. Maybe she wanted a little extra, and that's why she held up Charlie. We could maybe figure she and her man were in with the others. They maybe had spare horses waiting to give the gang a chance to get away. They probably got some of the loot for doing it."

"So why didn't they stay with the rest of them?" Henry asked.

Clinton answered that one. "If we'd caught up with the gang, they'd have been in the clear, unless one of them talked. And generally they don't tell tales out of school. It ain't anything heroic or romantic. It's just that if one outlaw tells on another, his days are numbered. No other outlaw will have anything to do with him, unless it's to give him a slug."

Mary Lou's soft voice cut through the silence that followed. "They kept clear until they were pretty sure we'd lost the trail, and then it was arithmetic all the way."

"Arithmetic?" Pearse asked.

"Division. Two into sixty thousand or so comes out a lot better than six into sixty thousand. Once they didn't get what they wanted from you, Charlie, they followed the others until they got a chance to take them."

"I would hate to live with that on my conscience," Henry said. "Money can't buy peace of mind."

"With some, it does," Krause muttered, and then they set to tracking by moonlight.

At daybreak they stopped for a couple of hours sleep, a cup of coffee, and some hardtack. They made a small fire to boil the coffee, and they put it out immediately.

Pearse guessed that Krause had put it together pretty well.

Mary Lou and Krause had taken care of the loose ends. If they were right, the gang had originally been six in number, and the couple who'd taken the black satchel from him had probably arranged for spare horses to ride when the other four ditched the stage. When they figured the others had a good start over any pursuit, they followed, keeping well to the side to hide their tracks. The rest was plain to see.

Offhand, Pearse guessed they'd head for Laramie or Cheyenne to get down to Denver, where they could convert the gold into greenbacks. But not too many well-dressed individuals could walk into a bank and turn over two hundred pounds of gold. At about sixteen dollars an ounce, that was about what it would weigh. He guessed they'd take some of the gold and hide the rest.

They followed the trail into the foothills, and then they lost it for a time in a ravine filled with loose gravel and rock. When they found it again, there were only two horses to follow.

Each of them had the same questions: Who had stayed, who had gone ahead? More to the point, where was the gold?

"We got a choice here," Clinton observed. "We can follow the two horses we know about, or we can backtrack and see what happened to the other two. It might slow us down some, but I say we look for the two that're missing."

Painstakingly they searched along the banks of the stream until they found a place where the dirt had been swept clear of prints with a pine branch. A little more searching revealed a canyon leading off to the north. There were tracks of four horses going in and tracks of two horses coming out.

"Let's have a look," Clinton ordered, and they rode in two abreast. Around the first bend in the canyon, they found the answer. Two horses lay dead in the fine sand. Their throats had been cut.

"He could have turned those horses loose," Krause muttered. "This is an animal."

They didn't have a lot of time to examine the dead horses, not that there was any need. A rifle shot boomed out, echoing from the rocky walls of the canyon. Pearse saw a curl of smoke from behind a boulder a hundred yards away just before he slid from the saddle and flattened himself on the ground.

For a moment it was quiet, and then another shot came whining overhead. Clinton fired twice with his Winchester, and Mary Lou and Pearse grabbed reins and led the horses back around the bend.

For a time there was silence. No shots, no voices. And then Clinton bellowed, "Come on out with your hands up!"

More silence. Whoever was behind the boulder wasn't going to be tricked into giving away his exact position. Pearse tried to think of what he'd do if the odds were one against five. One man had ridden off with the remaining two horses, leaving his partner to hold the fort. The man behind the rock would be in no frame of mind to fight. Given half a chance, he'd give up and blame his partner for everything.

Mary Lou touched Pearse on the arm. "Shouldn't we circle and get behind that boulder?"

"Probably. Wait here and I'll have a try." He groundhitched the horses he was holding and began the climb up the side of the canyon.

It wasn't a long climb, but it was a hard one. Rock kept slipping down, and for every foot he made, he lost half of it. Finally he got to the top and followed the edge of the canyon to where he could make out the boulder and see who was behind it.

The rifleman looked like nobody he'd ever seen, until he had a glimpse of auburn hair spilling out from under a wide-brimmed hat. She was sitting on a small rock behind the boulder, and several cartridge cases glinted in the fading light. She had been shooting at somebody beside the posse, and Pearse could guess who that had been. As Krause would have said, it didn't take a genius to figure that one out.

Chapter Eight

Pearse got to a place where he could cover the rock and the boulder at the same time, and then he yelled down to her. "You're covered! Lay down your guns and stand up!"

She flinched at the voice coming from the rear, but she started to turn around anyway. Pearse sent a slug into the sand five feet in front of her. "That's for openers," he called. "Now drop 'em!"

She tossed the rifle away. "Now stand up," he prompted. "And get rid of that Colt."

He couldn't see another gun on her, but he remembered the one she'd had in her pocket back in Deadwood, and he wasn't going to take chances with this lady. He had the edge, because she couldn't see him unless she turned around, and he didn't think she had the nerve to do that.

Clinton bawled out, "Is that you, Charlie?"

"It's me. Come on in, I've got her covered."

If Clinton was surprised, he didn't show it. He came walking in, Winchester on his hip, and he held it on her until he was maybe six feet away. "Charlie said to drop the other gun. I'd do that, if I was you."

"What's he going to do? Shoot me in the back?"

"If he has to, lady. If he has to."

The Navy Colt came out of her waistband and joined the rifle in the sand. Pearse hoped she didn't have another one tucked away in a boot or something. He scrambled down the side of the canyon and approached her from the rear, careful to stay out of Clinton's line of fire.

The others came in then, and Clinton motioned for her to go up to the bend in the canyon. She went willingly, and Pearse wondered if she hoped to get a gun from one of the saddle bags.

"That's far enough," Clinton said. "Now talk."

"Not to you, Marshal. Not to any man with you." And then she caught sight of Mary Lou. "How did you get here?"

Mary Lou smiled pleasantly, as if they had been two ladies about to take tea. "It would take too long to tell you. More to the point, how did you get here?"

"Go to hell."

"Me-oh-my. Such talk from a lady," Mary Lou admonished. "Now we know you took my clothes and money in Deadwood, and you and your friend held up Mr. Pearse. Why in the world did you want to do that, when you had a perfectly good stage to rob?"

The mystery woman pursed her mouth and spat. It didn't light before Mary Lou backhanded her with a left and punched her in the stomach with a right. "You're going to talk sooner or later," Mary Lou said. "You might as well start now."

Clinton stepped forward. "Don't abuse the prisoner," he said, but it was plain to see that he didn't much care so long as she talked.

"Her name's Ellen Murphy," Mary Lou said conversationally. "She was married to a captain over at Fort Robinson, and then she ran off with a no-good lieutenant who had his mind set on making big money. Name's Rodney Harris, and there's paper out on him."

They were open-mouthed at the revelation. Clinton was the first to recover. "How do you know all this?" he asked Mary Lou.

"My father was sutler at Fort Robinson for ten years. I grew up there." She grinned at Pearse. "Harris tried to get rich holding up a bank in Sioux Falls. According to the paper out on him, he only got about a thousand dollars. I guess that's when he figured stages were easier pickings."

"They weren't," Ellen Murphy said. "There was only about a hundred pounds of gold on it."

Clinton grinned. "So you knew about that. Keep talking."

He had her dead to rights, and she talked. The only hope she had was to tell what she knew. That and put the blame on the renegade lieutenant.

According to her, she and Harris had scouted out the stage to be robbed and told the rest of the gang how to handle it. One of them had heard a rumor that Reynolds was selling his share of the sutler's store, and that Mary Lou was going to Julesburg to get married and to deliver the money. Pearse guessed that despite Colonel's precautions word had got out, maybe through a rider's loose mouth, maybe from one of the hostlers.

She and Harris had sidetracked to pick up Colonel's money, and when they found out Mary Lou didn't have it in her hotel room, they waited for Pearse. And I obliged them, he thought.

"What a mess to wade through," Clinton said when she was done. "Now we got as far as you and Harris holding up Pearse here, taking his little black bag and running. What happened after that?"

"He fooled us," she admitted, and she gave Pearse a look that could kill. "He'd taken the money out of the bag, and we didn't find out until we stopped for the night. We were supposed to meet the others down the road at that stage station. This was all Rodney's doing. He planned the whole thing, and I had to go along with it. He'd have killed me."

Clinton nodded, as if nothing in the world was bothering him. "And then what did you do?"

It was a question she was going to have trouble answering, Pearse thought. If she said they'd gone to the little house, she was going to have to explain away two dead bodies. If she said nothing about the house, she was going to have to explain how she and Harris kept on the trail without stopping by the house.

"We followed them west," she said. "We were off to the side, and we didn't always have the tracks in sight, but Rodney knew they were headed for Laramie, so we just kept going west, and we picked up their trail just short of where they stopped for the night."

"And then?"

"Rodney said he was going to get closer and see what they were up to. He said they hadn't waited for us like they were supposed to do, and he guessed they were going to take the gold for themselves."

"He was probably right," Clinton said. She'd sidestepped a couple of murders pretty well, he thought. Her story wasn't perfect, but it cast some reasonable doubt on what had happened to the old couple down at the house.

"Rodney called in to them, saying who we were, and one of them went for his gun. Rodney shot him, and then the other three went for their guns and Rodney shot them too."

"Uh-huh. You're leaving out a little though."

She looked at him wide-eyed. "Not that I can recollect, no."

"All right, what happened after that?"

"Rodney rolled them up in their blankets, and then we took the pack horses and headed out. Rodney said we could go to Laramie ourselves and sell the gold. We kept going, and Rodney said to break trail, so we backtracked to the canyon here. And then when I wasn't watching close, he hit me and knocked me out. When I came to, the horses were dead and he had ridden away with the pack horses. I came back here, in case he changed his mind and came back to kill me." She looked at him helplessly. "That's all I know, and if he hadn't threatened to kill me, I wouldn't be in this mess."

Clinton turned to Mary Lou Reilly. "Watch her," he ordered.

He guessed even Pearse would have some second thoughts about manhandling a woman. But Miss Reilly would have no compunction about putting a slug through Miss Murphy if she had to.

He motioned to the others and led the way down toward the mouth of the canyon. "Well, what do you boys think?"

Tom Henry was the first to speak up. "I think she told the truth all the way to the stage station. After that, she's lying in her teeth."

"I'll go with Tom," Krause said. "The four of them went to the house and changed horses. Maybe they paid the old man, maybe it was an even trade. But they didn't have no reason to kill the old people. If they didn't kill the people on the stage they stole, why would they kill the people in that little house?"

"Well, who did?" Clinton asked. He wasn't arguing with

anybody, just absorbing information and making up his mind what to do next.

Pearse put in his two cents worth. "What probably happened was, Harris and his lady friend came along after the other four had left. The old man told him about the horse swapping, and Harris or the Murphy woman figured he might tell somebody else, so they shot them."

"Sounds about like it," Clinton said. "Why do you figure Murphy shot one of them?"

"Two different guns did the killing. The old lady was shot with a pistol, maybe that .36 the woman was toting. But the man was shot with something a whole lot bigger, maybe a rifle. You have to figure a shootist won't change guns in the middle of a gunfight. My guess is, Harris killed the old man and Murphy shot his wife. They wanted to keep them from telling anybody they were there."

"We'd have found out anyway," Tom Henry said. "They didn't have to kill them."

Alois Krause nodded. "They was buying time. But I seen some like that before. They like to kill people. Any reason is good enough for them."

Clinton nodded. "That about sums it up. Let's get on back and take care of business."

They filed back up the canyon to where Mary Lou Reilly held Ellen Murphy at gunpoint. Clinton thought she was enjoying the job. He didn't blame her.

"You're under arrest, Miss Murphy," he said. "There's a lot of holes in your story, but we'll get to the bottom of it later. Right now, we've got to catch up with your partner."

"I am innocent! Everything I did was because Rodney threatened to kill me if I didn't do what he said!"

"Like I said, you're under arrest. If it turns out you're telling the truth, you'll go free. If you want to be tied up, we can arrange that."

"I give you my word," Ellen Murphy said.

"Uh-huh. Take off your boots, and then I'll be sure."

She blushed, something Clinton would have thought she'd be incapable of, but she took off the boots and handed them over.

66

He turned to Mary Lou. "This here's a job for a woman. Search her and make sure she don't have some kind of weapon hid on her."

"I won't be touched," Ellen Murphy said. "I gave you my word I wouldn't try to escape."

"Not the same thing," Clinton said. "Search her, Miss Reilly. And watch her close. She's tricky."

Mary Lou did a good job of it, patting Murphy's pockets and picking her shirt open. She even took the pins out of her hair, and it was good that she did, because a little derringer came tumbling out.

"Something you forgot, I guess," Clinton smiled.

There were a couple of ways to go, Clinton thought. One would be to take Murphy with them, the other would be to send her back to Deadwood with Krause and Henry. If he took her along, she might very well warn Harris if she got within shouting distance. And there was no telling what damage she might do while they were distracted trying to find his mind.

"Tom, you and Alois can escort Miss Murphy back to Deadwood and put her in jail. I'll be along as soon as I can. I'll take Charlie and Miss Reilly with me, and we'll try to catch up with Mr. Harris."

Alois Krause was obviously unhappy with the idea. Well, like it or lump it, Clinton thought. "How are we going to manage without a horse for her? Unless we use one of the spares, that is."

"You can mount her on one of your spares," Clinton said. "The three of us are going to need ours."

"You want us to ride all the way up to Deadwood?" Henry asked him.

"No. Take her over to the stage station we stopped at and turn in the spare horse there. You can tie on behind and ride the stage with her. Keep her hands tied and watch her like a hawk. I want to find her in the jail when I get back."

"What's the charge?" Ellen Murphy said. "It's not legal to put me in jail without a charge."

"The charge is attempted murder and suspicion of murder," Clinton said. "Better get going while you still got light. Naturally you get paid until you get her in jail."

"Yah," Krause said. "That part of it I like."

They went through the saddle bags of the dead horses and found nothing of value. No gold, no weapons. Only a supply of jerky they shared out and a couple of horseshoes nobody wanted.

Mary Lou went back up the canyon and retrieved the Winchester Murphy had dropped and the Navy Colt. She stuck the Colt in her saddle bag and tied the rifle by its saddle ring to a thong on her saddle. Clinton watched with approval. She knew what she was doing. He'd miss Alois's tracking skill, but he guessed Pearse was pretty good himself. And Mary Lou Reilly could handle herself in a pinch. She'd proved that.

Clinton watched the three riders until they were out of sight behind one of the green hills. Then he, Pearse, and Mary Lou followed the tracks of Harris's three horses.

It went that way until they came over a saddle and found another little stream, and then the tracks went into the water and stopped. Pearse swore mildly, and Clinton echoed his sentiments. "This here's a cagey coon," he said. "Point bothers me is why he's being so dang careful. For all he knows, we lost the trail a long time back."

Mary Lou smiled. "That's why he's where he is, and that's why we're where we are. If I was on the run, I'd do the same thing, wouldn't you?"

Clinton nodded. "It never hurts to be too careful. Let's head upstream and see what we can find."

"Suppose one of us goes downstream too. That way, we've got him whatever way he jumps," Pearse said.

Three miles upstream they found the tracks. Harris had led the horses out of the water on a strip of shingle, and they had left only scars on the rock in a couple of places, but Clinton dismounted and went up the bank. He found where they'd scrambled up and Harris had tried to brush away the tracks. That was a dead giveaway, because nobody'd bother hiding tracks unless he knew somebody was after him.

"Think you'll be all right if I leave you here and go fetch Charlie?" Clinton asked.

"I'll be fine," Mary Lou assured him. "He's probably quit looking by now, and he'll be on his way back."

"I hope so," Clinton grumbled. "That's a lot of riding for a tired horse. And we're burning daylight. Not that there's much of that left."

She smiled at him. "Don't worry. If we don't catch up with Mr. Harris, we can be sure he'll be waiting for us at Julesburg."

When Clinton was out of sight, she dismounted and eased the girth on the horse she'd ridden, and then she transferred the rifle to the saddle on the spare horse. If she had to ride for it, she wanted a fresh mount.

Carefully she watered the horses in the stream, one at a time, and filled her canteen. It was growing darker now, but she wasn't worried. Charlie Pearse wasn't the kind to run off and leave a job undone. And he was smart enough to have quit looking after a couple of miles.

She thought about making a fire and rejected the idea. If Colonel had been here, he wouldn't have, and that was good enough for her. Just about everything she'd ever learned about plainscraft she'd learned from Pa or from Colonel. She wished Colonel was here now. He'd be good company, and she bet he'd be extra good company if they got a chance to be alone.

Not that he'd ever touched her in that way. Colonel was a patient man, and he was too good a friend of her father not to behave honorably toward his daughter. Now Pa was dead, but that made no never-mind. Colonel was still an honorable man.

She heard the horses before she saw them, and she untied the rifle and stood apart from her own horses. Harris would probably be making tracks for Cheyenne by now, but you never knew. He was as tricksy in his own way as Ellen Murphy in hers.

But the horses were the ones ridden by Charlie and the Marshal, and she didn't deny that she was glad to see them.

"Nothing happening here," she told them. "I watered the horses and filled my canteen. I guess that's about all."

Clinton nodded. "You done just fine. I just wish I knew what the devil he wants to do next. I could've sworn he'd head for Laramie, but he might have struck out for Cheyenne."

"If there was nobody after him," she said. "But he knows it's only a matter of time, and then he's stuck between the rock and the hard place. I'd say he wants to put a lot of distance between him and us until he can get rid of the gold. Either sell it or hide it."

Pearse nodded his approval. "Let me make a guess. He knows something we haven't been thinking about. He knows about the little package I have to deliver to Colonel Reynolds. Probably Murphy told him all about it. And it's paper money you can spend any place. He can hide the loot from the stage and wait until it's safe to go back for it, so long as he can pick up Colonel's money."

"Oh, hell," Clinton said. "Excuse me, miss. Of course that's it. He's going to hide the gold, because that's a good bargaining point if he gets caught. And then he's going to turn the horses loose and take a stagecoach like a gentleman. He ain't even going to bother looking for you two, because he knows you got to come to him. All he has to do is be in Julesburg when you get there."

"Why's he going to get horses?" she asked.

"To break trail," Clinton said. "He figures if the impossible happens and we follow him as far as the stage route, he'll be able to hide himself among the other passengers."

"There's one thing he's probably not figuring on," Pearse grinned. "When he gets to Julesburg, there's going to be three of us."

Mary Lou saw the flash of Pearse's teeth in the gloom, and she thought there was a ruthlessness about the man she hadn't noticed before. She was glad he was chasing Harris and not her. He was the kind of man Pa used to say was the best friend in the world or the worst kind of enemy, and it was up to you to decide which one he would be.

Chapter Nine

It was still early, but the light was gone and they were too tired to go on. There was no sense killing themselves, Clinton said, and Pearse agreed.

Mary Lou announced that she felt crawly and that she was going to take a bath in the river. It sounded like a good idea, and Clinton and Pearse sat on the ground and munched hardtack and jerky while they waited for her. A fire was out of the question, because for all they knew Harris might be watching his backtrail for smoke.

When Mary Lou came back with dripping hair and damp clothes, Pearse and Clinton took their turns at washing the trail dust away. The water was medium cold, and it rested them almost as much as a good sleep would have done.

They lay back on the ground and waited for the moon to come up, and then they set out again, following the tracks they could see, guessing when they lost them. By and large they led in the direction of a stage station Pearse remembered, one stage to the south of the one where they'd questioned the agent.

There was nothing like getting to the right place at the wrong time, Pearse thought, unless it was getting to the wrong place at the wrong time. They found the station without too much trouble, but it was the one south of the one they'd aimed at, and they were just in time to see the stage disappear into the moon-light. A short conversation with a sleepy agent produced the news that there had been a tall gentleman matching Harris's description aboard.

"If that don't beat the Dutch," Clinton said. "I don't guess there's even a telegraph here."

"Closest one's in Cheyenne," the agent offered. "But I don't guess anybody'd be awake this time of night."

"Let's ketch some sleep," Clinton grunted. "We'll figure it out what to do in the morning."

But nobody had any good ideas by the time the sun got them up. Harris had gotten another good head start on them, and there was nothing much they could do about it, short of cutting across country, a dry country at that, and with tired horses.

Mary Lou wondered what he had done with the gold. "He sure didn't climb aboard a stage with two hundred pounds of nuggets."

"He probably cached it somewheres," Clinton guessed. "And Murphy said there wasn't that much."

"She was lying about that too," Mary Lou said. "Couldn't you tell?"

"Maybe yes, maybe no," Pearse frowned. "There's no way he could have found the time to hide it, unless he hid it back where we found the lady. He could have ridden out half an hour and stuck it under a rock."

Clinton wasn't worried about the gold. "What I think is, we better get our hands on that fellow, and then we can find out from him where he put the gold. And the only way we're going to do that is to get to Julesburg."

"We don't have to worry about that," Mary Lou said. "He'll wait for us."

Clinton gave her a dirty look for her pains. Pearse grinned.

They bought feed for the horses, and then they followed the stage route the rest of the way to Cheyenne, because Clinton wanted to send a telegram to Deadwood and partly because none of them wanted to make a long ride through the Sand Hills. Even the jackrabbits had a hard time finding a living in the Sand Hills, and they were all tired of hard riding and cold jerky.

Cheyenne was an up-and-coming town. It had cattle money to rely on, and even if the luxuries came high, the necessities were reasonable. They got rooms at the Cattleman's Hotel—on the house because Clinton had them on the payroll—and they ate a good hot dinner in the dining room: oysters and steak and snap beans and prairie chicken, with a peach cobbler to finish. After that, Clinton went off in search of a telegraph office, and Pearse escorted Mary Lou to the Ladies Lounge.

Pearse didn't know who Clinton was going to send a telegram to, but he hoped it was to somebody who knew something about what they were doing or supposed to be doing. By this time, he wasn't too sure of what was going on. Whatever it was, he hoped it wasn't going to interfere with their getting to Julesburg where he could deliver Mary Lou and Colonel's twenty thousand dollars.

While Clinton was off sending his telegram and Mary Lou was looking out of place in the Ladies Lounge, dressed as she was in men's trail clothes, Pearse took the opportunity to check the flour sack. He hadn't paid it too much mind during the riding, because there were more important things to do, like keeping from being ambushed, but now there was time and a private place to count it out.

It was all there, which was not too surprising, since it had been escorted by three lawmen. But lawmen had been known to turn crooked too, especially where a lot of money was at stake.

Clinton came into the bar looking mad enough to tackle a den of rattlesnakes. Krause and Henry had delivered Miss Murphy to the Deadwood jail with strict orders to keep a good watch on her because she was a suspect in a murder. Six murders, as a matter of fact.

Then they had gone off to do what any sensible man would do: get a bath and clean clothes and sleep around the clock. When they got around to check on the jailhouse, they were told that Miss Murphy was still sleeping. At least, that was what the jailer told them, and he was a mite put out when they insisted on checking.

"Tom Henry got suspicious right off," Clinton growled. "They went on back to her cell, and she was gone. She'd pulled the blankets over the straw tick, which she bunched up, and she pried a couple of bars apart with a board she ripped off the bunk." He paused and took a long swig of rock-and-rye. "The worst of it was, she bent the damn bars back so nobody could tell she was gone unless they pulled up the blankets."

Pearse shook his head. "Ingenious, wasn't she?"

"What in hell is that?"

"Slippery, Marshal. Slippery as water on old ice."

Clinton passed that one by. "Where's our friend?"

"I left her in the Ladies Lounge. Wonder what she'll make of all this."

Clinton fetched a telegram from his pocket. "Murphy made a dummy, bent bars with board, and got through. Bent bars back again," it read.

A young fellow in trail clothes with a hat pulled down over his face walked into the bar. Pearse stared for a moment and then he smiled. "What's your pleasure, partner?"

"Rock-and-rye," Mary Lou said. "It sure got boring in there. Anybody ever tell you gents that men have more fun than women?"

Pearse shrugged. "Reckon it all depends on the woman."

Clinton got out the telegram again and showed it to Mary Lou. "This is about all I needed to make my night complete."

She shook her head in wonderment. "That woman is capable of anything, isn't she?"

"It sometimes happens," Pearse said. "I one time put two sidewinders in jail, and the jailer's helper let himself get hit on the head with a thunder mug. They got loose with a couple of the town marshal's guns. It's kind of funny now, but I damn near got killed over it."

Clinton was interested. "What happened to them?" he wanted to know. It was a professional interest.

"They hunted me until they found me, and I shot them both."

Mary Lou was wide-eyed. "Dead?"

"About as dead as you'd want," Pearse said. "It was better them than me. They killed my girl."

Clinton looked satisfied. Justice had been done.

Mary Lou sipped at her drink. "This is downright interesting," she said. "I always mistrusted those skinny women. They was either out for somebody else's man or they'd already caught him."

"Could be it'll work out for the best," Clinton guessed. "If I got it straight, she'll be hunting Mr. Harris just the way we will."

"How's she going to get clothes and money?" Pearse wondered. "She won't get far without a gun, either."

Mary Lou chuckled. "Why, the same way she always has, Charlie. She'll sweet-talk some man, and he'll be fool enough to stake her, or she'll steal what he's got. And a lot of men are so worried about being men, they won't say a word about it."

"Sounds like you knew the lady pretty well," Clinton said. It was as close as he could come to asking a question without being nosey.

"Pretty well. Her daddy was a major, and she thought she was God's gift to the human race. My pa was only the sutler, you see. Never mind that he made a lot more money than her pa, she acted like *she* was the major. Then she got married to a captain, and it wasn't too long before she started taking up with other men. Colonel was one of them for a time, and then she got rid of him in short order to take up with Harris, and they ran off together. Colonel was broken-hearted for a while, and then he got some sense. He'd been making some money playing poker, and he invested in my pa's store. About that time, Colonel and I came to an agreement.

"When he quit the Army and went to Julesburg to trade horses, he left his money in Pa's business. But Pa died three months ago, and that's where the money came from, the money you're taking to Colonel."

"Makes sense," Clinton said. "That's how our Miss Murphy knew about the money to be had for the taking, and that's how Harris found out about it."

It all proved to Pearse that if a man could make a fool of himself over a woman, it worked the other way too. Harris had taken advantage of Miss Murphy, and maybe he'd had that in mind all along. Or maybe true love had gone sour.

"The thing is," Pearse mused, "we still got the same problem: how to get Mary Lou and the money to Colonel without somebody getting killed along the way."

"Money," Clinton said reflectively. "I don't want to tend your business, having enough of my own to take care of, but was I you, I'd go to a bank here and deposit it in Reynolds's name. You could get a letter of credit to your bank over in Julesburg, and maybe you could get Mary Lou here to take it."

It was such a simple idea, Pearse wondered why he hadn't thought of it before. Of course Colonel had said he didn't want a letter of credit, but circumstances had changed. And if Pearse put it in his name, he could present it at the Julesburg bank and draw out the money from his account and give it to Colonel.

The next morning, Pearse went down the street to the bank and talked to a vice-president. Half-an-hour's talk with the man convinced him that that was the way to go. Pearse explained to him that Colonel didn't want the money in his own name and that he, Pearse, was in some danger.

The banker came up with the solution. "If there's someone in Julesburg you can trust, put it in his name. You hold the letter, and you can go to the bank with him and draw out the cash. Then you can give it to your reluctant friend."

Pearse put the money in John Carrington's name, since he was the Sheriff and had stood by him when they'd ridden after the Shooter. When he got to Julesburg, Pearse guessed he could explain it to the banker so nobody'd get the notion that the Sheriff was a rich man.

When Pearse left the bank, he felt a hundred pounds lighter. Now all he had to worry about was getting Mary Lou to Julesburg in one piece. And himself, for that matter.

When he got back to the hotel, Clinton and Mary Lou were waiting for him in the lobby.

"Horses ready?" Pearse asked.

"We're selling them, unless we can dicker a ride for them in a cattle car," Clinton said. "We'll take the railroad to the first stop east of Julesburg, and then we'll come into town from there. Harris can't cover the whole dang town."

"I hope not," Pearse said. "I surely hope not."

Chapter Ten

Pearse had heard that back East the locomotives had straight stacks instead of bell-shaped ones. It was a new wrinkle, he guessed. But this wasn't the East, and their locomotive under the new paint looked like it might have come straight out of the War Between The States. Maybe it had.

Marshal Clinton showed his badge and got permission to put their horses on a cattle car, and then they settled down in a coach with wooden seats. It beat riding, and since there wasn't much traffic, they each took a seat and stretched out full-length, on the sound principle that you never knew where your next sleep was coming from, so you might as well catch up on it while you had a chance.

Darkness came up to meet them as they chuffed their way east, and it was a while before the moon came up enough to see anything outside. Clinton produced a flask of pretty fair bourbon to help pass the time, and they cut it with water from the cooler at the end of the car.

The other two passengers kept themselves to themselves, as Mary Lou put it. The one was an elderly lady with an old-fashioned carpetbag, and the other was a drummer of some sort. The drummer had a display suitcase labeled "Jones and Company." He held it under his legs as if it contained a fortune. Maybe it did. It reminded Pearse of the burden he'd shed at the bank.

"Funny thing," Clinton reflected. "Five, ten years ago, we might have been held up by buffalo. Now, a feller'd be hard put to find one old bull and a couple of cows."

"Pretty much a thing of the past," Pearse said. "The hunters shot them to get money, and all along it was government policy to kill them off so the honyokers could come in with their plows and bust up good land could be used for grazing."

"That and it took away food for the Indians. They had no choice after that but to come on the reservations and live on government supplies or starve."

Mary Lou sat up and yawned. She was still wearing the men's clothes Pearse had bought her in Rapid City, and she looked mighty fetching. Pearse hoped Colonel would appreciate what he was getting.

"It's progress," she said. "Think of all the towns that are going to be here some day. Churches and stores and people living together without fighting. Farmers planting crops and not having to worry about buffalo trampling them down. Nobody worrying about keeping his scalp."

Clinton snorted. "They could've left it the way it was, for all of me. Take a look at the country once you get east of Ellsworth, and there's weeds instead of tall grass. If you ask me, the dang farmers are ruining some mighty fine cattle country. The whole problem with the United States is, there's too dang many people in them."

Pearse agreed with Clinton, but he didn't bother saying so. It seemed to him that something pretty wonderful was passing before his eyes, and that when the change was over, nobody'd want to live here unless he was a farmer or a storekeeper. He didn't worry about being out of a livelihood. Where there were people, there'd be gambling, and a good poker player could always make himself a respectable living if he didn't get greedy.

"It must be a small train," Mary Lou said. "I only counted one other coach and three cattle cars."

"I guess some of the rush to go west is over," Pearse said. "The gold is still there in the Black Hills and in Colorado, and there's plenty of silver to be had for the taking, but a few men are getting rich and the rest of them are barely making a living. Word must have got back somehow."

"A good thing," Clinton grumbled. "There's some damn fools in this world who'd kill themselves looking for a fortune when they could make a good living with ordinary hard work six days a week back where they come from."

"If it was all that good, Marshal, they'd have stayed back east." Mary Lou had the last word.

Feet stamped overhead and brake wheels squealed. The brakeman was setting the brakes in preparation for a stop.

The train came into the station with a wheeze of exhaust steam. There was a water tower filled by a windmill, a stack of cordwood beside the track, and a little shack.

"Taking on water and wood," Clinton explained. "The dang railroads are going to ruin this country."

"What are you going to do when you quit being Marshal?" Pearse asked.

"Head for the mountains, I guess. There's always going to be poker players, Charlie, and there's always going to be a need for lawmen. But I surely don't want to retire as a town constable in a little farming town. There's no excitement in it."

"Not much pay, either."

"There's that, too. But the main reason anybody goes into my line of work is because he feels he's doing some gcod keeping the skunks from preying on the honest citizens. Take that away, and there's no fun in living."

"It's dangerous work," Mary Lou said.

"It is, but where's the sense in living until you're so dang old you can't take care of yourself any more?"

Pearse heard the rattle of the chute being drawn up, but wood was still thunking into the tender. The fueling of the train was taking a long time, it seemed to him, but he hadn't ridden more than three or four trains in his whole life. For a man who spent the end of his boyhood living on the plains with a rifle and a horse to make his living when he wasn't learning the finer points of poker playing, that was about three or four too many. The last train he'd ridden was a Santa Fe from Denver to Wallace, and that was a good hundred miles south of the Union Pacific line they were on.

"There's two men getting on," Mary Lou announced.

Pearse and Clinton looked out the window. They were pretty shabby specimens, Pearse thought. One of them had an old blue Army shirt on, the other had a checked shirt. Both wore canvas pants and boots that looked like they'd started life in some quartermaster's warehouse.

"Deserters, more than likely," Clinton speculated. "They're getting on the car behind us."

"I hear maybe two out of ten men never finish their hitch," Pearse said.

Mary Lou snickered. "Make that three out of ten, and you'll be closer to the mark, Charlie. I grew up on an Army post."

"Did you notice was there an express car on this train?" Clinton asked. "I thought there was, but I'm not sure of it."

"Don't know," Pearse said. "But I can find out." He walked up the aisle to the front of the coach and opened the door. Sure enough, there was an express car he hadn't counted before.

"Uh-huh," Clinton said. "Strikes me that any man deserting the Army would want to head west to get into the mining business. He sure as the devil wouldn't want to go east and work for four dollars a week sweeping streets."

"They had saddle guns," Mary Lou said. "And sixguns too."

"That too," Clinton said. "A man going east could sell a sixgun for more here than he could there, unless he figured he might have a use for it along the way."

Pearse nodded. "Think they might try to hold up the train?"

"It's possible," Clinton said.

"They didn't have horses either," Mary Lou added. "How did they get to the station?"

"Another point," Pearse suggested. "No man in his right mind would go walking around the countryside in cavalry boots. And neither one of them looked to have sore feet."

Clinton looked at him shrewdly. "I can see how you're such a good poker player, Charlie. You pay attention to details."

"What do you think we ought to do about it?" Mary Lou asked. She was being her usual practical self, not trying to put anybody down the way some folks did.

"What I think is, we ought to get our tails off this train at the next stop and head across country. It won't be that much longer a ride, and the last thing I want to do is get mixed up in something that'll keep us from catching that skunk Harris."

"Amen to that," Pearse said.

"Let's sit over near the door," Mary Lou suggested. "That way we can get off faster if we have to."

Clinton nodded and they moved back in the coach. They'd picked seats in the center because it was a more comfortable ride between the wheels than it was over them, but being near the door had its advantages. If the two men who had boarded the train were going to hold up the passengers, they'd be in a better position to resist. Pearse approved.

"Don't be too obvious," Clinton said, "but now's the time to have your gun handy. Something don't smell too good about this, and I don't want to get caught with my britches down, like the feller says."

Mary Lou smiled. A lot of women would have got on their high horse at the word "britches," but Pearse guessed she'd lived around rough men long enough to know that there was no harm in calling a thing by its rightful name.

The locomotive huffed and wheezed and got about its job of pulling the train. The water tank and the wood crib slipped by slowly, and then the train picked up speed, and pretty soon they were rocketing down the track at a good clip, maybe thirty or forty miles an hour.

"Kind of makes a feller wonder," Clinton muttered. "Where in hell—'scuse me, Mary Lou—these folks are going that's so dang important they can't wait a little longer to get there."

Pearse chuckled. "Why, to Julesburg to catch Harris." Clinton laughed. "You got to admit I'm right, Marshal."

"I admit it, Charlie."

The brakeman had run up the train releasing the brakes with the brakewheels before the train had pulled out, but now there were footsteps overhead, running up to the front of the train. It was something to do with the train, Pearse guessed, but he hadn't been on enough trains to know what was right and what wasn't.

From the caboose, they heard somebody turning the brake wheel with a series of squeaks, and then he came forward and turned another wheel.

"Something's wrong," Clinton said. "We don't have a stop here that I know of."

Pearse guessed. "Maybe it's a hot box." Once in a while the boxes over the axles overheated, and the tallow and tow that lubricated the axles caught fire, and then the train had to be stopped until the fire went out and the box could be repacked.

Clinton made up his mind. "And maybe not. Charlie, get turned around to cover the rear door while I go up front to see what's going on. Shoot if you have to."

Pearse nodded and walked to the rear of the car, gun in hand. He positioned himself next to the door, so that whoever came in would have to look around to see him.

The train ground to a halt, and the conductor came through the door Pearse was guarding. "Nothing to worry about, folks. We got a little problem with the train, but we'll have it fixed in short order."

He didn't look like a man faced with an ordinary occurrence, Pearse thought. He looked more like a man scared out of his wits. Some of it was because he was the man in charge of the train. If he was wrong about something, he could lose his job. "What's wrong exactly?" Pearse wanted to know.

"Why nothing, sir."

"Where's the two fellows got on last stop?"

"Back in the other car. Now just take your seat, and everything'll be all right."

Pearse shouldered past him and looked in the other coach. The five passengers who had been there at the last stop were still there, but there was no sign of the two men.

Something creaked at the front of the coach, and Pearse recognized it as the sound of a linch-pin being pulled. The pin on the rear of one car dropped into a round link on the front of the car behind it, and when the train started, the front car pulled the rear car with it. What Pearse had heard was somebody uncoupling the express car from the rear part of the train.

Clinton appeared in the front doorway of the coach. He had his gun in one hand, his other hand held his coat open to display his badge. "U. S. Marshal," he said. "I want everybody out of this car now. Go to the rear car and get down on the floor." He nodded toward Pearse. "This man is my deputy. We'll handle the situation."

The elderly lady and the drummer raced each other to see who could get through the door first. The lady won by a bustle.

"Charlie, I think they've taken the locomotive and the tender and the express car. If that's all they're after, it'll be fine." Clinton shooed the conductor ahead of him into the rear car and told the passengers to get down on the floor. They looked their disbelief, but they obeyed him, either because of the badge or because of the six-gun in his hand.

Mary Lou stayed in the center of the forward coach, crouched down, gun in hand. She was watching the passengers through the doorway just in case any of them had ideas. Clinton took the front door, and Pearse walked past him to the first cattle car.

There didn't seem to be anybody about, so he stuck the Starr in his holster and climbed the ladder to the top of the car. He checked between the cars as he went back, but no one was hiding there. He risked a peek to the front and saw the locomotive and tender and the express car rolling down the track.

They were stranded somewhere in eastern Colorado, but at least the cattle car with their horses was still with the rest of the train.

The caboose was empty, except for the brakeman. He was lying on the floor with a knot on the side of his head as big as a walnut. Pearse checked the bunks and the privy to make sure nobody was hiding there, and then he bent down beside the brakeman. The man was breathing, and when Pearse felt his head, he couldn't find anything broken. He got water from the cooler in the corner and poured it on his head, and the brakeman came back from wherever he'd been. "Who in hell are you?" he wanted to know.

"I'm helping a U. S. Marshal. What happened?"

"A couple of shooters came through the door while I was having coffee and told me to set the brakes." He groaned. "This hurts like hell."

Pearse poured another cup of cold water over his head.

"I told them no, and one of them laid his gun barrel alongside my head. And that is all I know about it."

Pearse grinned. "You were damn lucky they didn't shoot you. You'll feel better in a little while. Soak a rag in cold water and hold it on that knot."

Somewhere in the distance there was a dull thud. "They blowed the express car," the brakeman said.

"Anything in it?"

"I doubt it. A lot of bother over nothing."

"Got a gun?"

The brakeman nodded. "Up in my bunk. I better get it in case they come back."

Pearse left the man to his sore head and his caboose and went back to the coaches. This time he walked alongside the tracks. If the robbers decided to back the locomotive and try their hand at robbing passengers, he'd make a smaller target.

Clinton was between cars peering to the front where the locomotive had stopped. "Anything, Charlie?"

Pearse told him about the brakeman and the two men who'd taken him, and Clinton grunted. "Might've guessed," he said. "I stopped to check out the horses, and by the time I caught on, they had the express car uncoupled and they were on their way. There's about five thousand on that express car, and that ought to keep them happy. I suppose there's three or four of them up ahead was waiting with horses and blasting powder."

Pearse's field glasses were still in the saddlebag in the cattle car, but even without them he could see the stalled engine, a little fume of smoke coming from the stack. Some little dots that were men were busy loading horses. He counted seven, which meant that five men had been waiting. Maybe less, if they'd used a horse to pack out the loot.

"Want to do anything about it?" he asked Clinton.

"Nothing we can do that ain't being done right now. By the time we got the horses out, they'd be out of sight. And the conductor's up a pole with a telegraph key. He's telegraphing east and to Cheyenne to let them know about it."

"Sounds like it's all taken care of," Pearse said. "I suggest we get our horses off this contraption and ride the rest of the way. If the crew's all right, we can take out from here."

"It hurts me to see those bastards get away," Clinton said. "I guess we could use the spare horses and mount up some of the passengers and take out after them."

"Maybe we could put the old lady on a horse."

Clinton glared at him. "I guess you think you're funny."

Pearse chuckled. "We could let somebody else take care of this and go after Harris ourselves," he said. "I never once saw a coyote chase two rabbits in two different directions and catch either one."

Clinton didn't thank Pearse for reminding him of the job ahead. "Well, let's not stand around here waiting for the millenium. I'll go get the lady and you can start getting them horses off."

Chapter Eleven

By the time they got the horses unloaded, the engine was chuffing its way back to the rest of the train. They stood by and watched, partly to make sure none of the robbers had changed his mind and come back to relieve the passengers of their valuables, and partly just to watch the proceedings.

The brakeman had recovered enough to guide the pin into the coupling of the front cattle car, and in a couple of minutes the train was hooked up again. The baggage car had a big hole in the side, and when they looked in, the safe door was off and the inside of the safe was bare. Pearse was reminded of the Chinese man who kept burning down houses to roast his pig. He'd read that somewhere in a book, and it had stuck with him.

While Clinton and Mary Lou finished gaping at the hole in the side of the boxcar, Pearse hunted up the conductor and learned that they were about forty miles west of Julesburg and maybe a tad to the north. To get there, all they'd have to do was follow the tracks.

But that might not be too healthy, all things considered. Harris would surely be watching for trains. He told Clinton he didn't think it would be too smart.

"There's such a thing as being over-cautious, Charlie."

"Better safe than sorry. Harris isn't dumb, and he's going to be prowling around town checking the roads. He's going to be watching for us, and he's going to shoot first if we give him half a chance."

"How are you going to get into Julesburg? Wait until he dies of old age?"

"I'm not going in."

"How are you going to deliver that letter of credit to your friend? Have a little carrier pigeon drop it in?"

Pearse smiled. "I've got a friend has a ranch about twenty miles the other side of Julesburg, and he can deliver it. Nobody would suspect him, and Harris doesn't know him from Adam. He can take the letter to Colonel without anyone the wiser."

"And Harris goes scot free, Charlie?"

"I got a job to do," Pearse said. "That is delivering the lady and the money to Colonel. You help me with my job, and I'll help you with yours."

"You're still deputized," Clinton reminded him.

Mary Lou cleared her throat. "That reminds me. You never gave me a badge, Marshal."

"Ladies don't get to be deputies."

"Be honest—I earned it. I took the same risks Charlie did, and I've got no legal standing. Now, if you deputized me, everything would be above board and nice and legal."

"How in the devil would I explain deputizing a female?"

Pearse interrupted. "She's right, Clinton. You could just give her a badge and sign her on as M. L. Reilly. That would keep everything clean and neat."

Clinton growled. "I never seen anything like this. I guess you're one of these here feminists."

"Just your deputy, Marshal," Mary Lou smiled. "Now how about it?"

Clinton knew when he was licked. He reached in his saddle bag and hauled out a dented star with U. S. Marshal on it. He handed it to Mary Lou. "Raise your right hand and repeat after me."

Mary Lou smiled sweetly. "Thank you, Marshal. Now I feel all official-like."

"Now can we get down to serious business? I'd like to get to Julesburg and nail that critter and take him back to Deadwood to the bar of justice."

Pearse guessed that what he really meant was that he'd rather go into Julesburg and have the shootdown and get it over with. But with a man like Harris, that was a good way to get yourself killed. Pearse didn't know about Clinton, but he figured he was a little young to die.

"Well, Marshal? You going to help us?"

"I have been, Charlie, I have been. All right, we'll do it your way. But we got to get Harris behind bars, one way or another. The man's a murderer, and he's got to be brought before the bar of justice."

He said the words something like a preacher giving the sermon of his lifetime, like they had come out of Holy Writ. With a man like that, Pearse thought, you sometimes had a hard time making him see things the way they were.

"You're not going to do it getting yourself killed. Harris is a dangerous man, and you better take it easy and make sure of what you're doing before you go barging in."

"And get you killed. Right, Charlie?"

"That too. I'm no hero, and I don't aim to make a name for myself, but I can stand up like any man when the occasion calls for it."

"And you'll help me get Harris?"

"We both will," Mary Lou said. "And Colonel too."

Clinton nodded, and then they mounted and rode off down the railroad track, keeping to the ballast where the riding would be easier. Pearse figured they could put in thirty miles or so before they'd cut off to the north and head for the Thatcher ranch. It would take longer, but Mary Lou and the letter of credit would be safe and in one piece when they got there.

Three hours later, they saw the smoke of a west-bound train, and Pearse knew it was time to leave the track and head directly to the ranch. It was sad to see the smoke, because it reminded him of the changes that had occurred since he had grown up in the big, beautiful plains country.

The future was catching up with him, and like Clinton, he wasn't so sure he liked it. It meant that the east, with all its put-on airs and its fancy ways of living, was coming out to take over.

Some day he'd think to tell somebody how he'd once fought off wolves by shooting the leader at three hundred yards with a

Sharps Big Fifty, and they'd look at him as if he was stretching the truth. Or even worse, they wouldn't know what the hell he was talking about.

The ranch was at the end of a long valley, and they came in from the west, hitting the valley about a mile north of the ranch. They sat the horses to give them a breather, and Pearse looked down the valley to where a couple of cowboys were driving a herd of cows up-valley toward the summer range. Pearse thought one of them might have been Jesse Pense, whom he'd ridden with the summer before, but it was too far away to tell and he was too lazy to get out the field glasses and make sure.

Everything looked peaceful down at the ranch, so they rode in, leading the spare horses behind them. When they got around to the front, Pearse helloed the house, and Molly Thatcher came out to see who it was. That was another sign of the times, Pearse thought: even two years ago, she'd have had a gun in her hand if she came out at all.

Molly set out a bowl of doughnuts and poured coffee, and they all got comfortable. Jim was off at the south range, she said, and she told them that he was considering fencing in some of the land.

"It's better for breeding," she told them. "You can keep the good stock away from the scrubs. Besides, it's a good way to protect our springs."

Pearse could see where fences could cause more trouble than they were worth, but he let it ride.

Clinton didn't. "Some folks might want to get to that water, and they wouldn't care who they run over to get there. You could have a range war on your hands."

"We can handle it," Molly Thatcher said shortly.

"Wonder what Colonel's thinking now," Mary Lou chuckled. "I bet he's wondering if you ran off with me and the money, Charlie."

"Lord, I hope not. Last thing I need is Colonel mad at me. I got enough people wanting a strip of my hide without him."

Jim Thatcher came in half an hour later. He was in a good mood the way a man should be when he had a good herd, good land, and a pretty missus and good hands. "How's it going, Charlie?"

Pearse made the introductions and told him what they needed.

"I can't see any problem. I go to town and put up my horse at the livery stable, and then I walk around a little and find the Sheriff and hand him this envelope. Is that it?"

"That's all there is to it," Pearse said.

"And then the Sheriff goes to the bank and gets cash and takes it over to Colonel."

"That's it, Jim."

"And nobody's going to wonder what a Sheriff who works for seventy-five dollars a month is doing with a whole wagonload of money? Come on, Charlie!"

"Let 'em wonder. I could do it myself, but Harris knows me by sight, and he'll be waiting for me to show up."

"One thing you haven't figured on," Jim Thatcher said. "Harris knows Colonel by sight too, and the minute he sees Carrington come out of that bank with a package and head for the stable, he's going to wonder. He might get to wondering enough to go on in and take the money and kill whoever stands in his way.

"I hadn't thought of that," Pearse admitted.

"He knows me too," Mary Lou said.

Clinton shook his head. "Charlie, it looks like you complicated things a little bit more than you ought to have."

"Meaning it's up to me to get them uncomplicated?"

"You said it, friend. I didn't."

Pearse sipped at his coffee. It bought him a little time. Not much. "Let's take care of some easy stuff first. Jim? I want to give you back your horse and pick up mine. I got an extra out there you can have for your trouble."

Jim Thatcher nodded. "Fair enough. You want that Sharps back too, I guess?

"Uh-huh. I'll take that and my bay horse and be on my way."

"I'm going with you," Clinton said. "Looks to me like you could use a sidekick. Besides, it's my job to bring Harris in."

"You got me too," Mary Lou reminded him.

"No, I ain't," Clinton told her. "You stay right here until Colonel can come for you. Otherwise, you'll complicate things."

"Don't complicate," Pearse said. "The Marshal doesn't like complications." He figured he'd give Clinton back some of his complicating talk. For one thing, he'd been the one to suggest the letter of credit, not Pearse. For another, Pearse hadn't really made things any worse than they were.

But the real truth of the matter was, Pearse didn't feel too enthused about riding into a town where a fast gun was waiting for him. He didn't feel like killing a man he'd only met once, and he sure as hell didn't feel like getting killed.

But there was nothing else to do. The minute Carrington went in that bank and came out with a bundle to take to the livery stable, Harris was going to know about it. And Colonel and Carrington and maybe Jim Thatcher could wind up dead.

"Harris," he said. "Does he know you?"

Clinton shook his head. "Not that I know of."

"Then you stay clear of me. If he sees anybody with me, he's going to act first and worry about it afterwards."

"You ain't going in there alone," Clinton said. "There is no way in the world I am going to let you walk into something you can't handle."

"I can handle it. I'm still a deputy marshal, right?"

Clinton nodded reluctantly.

"All right. I'll go in tonight and give the letter of credit to the Sheriff and explain the situation. Then I'll find Colonel and tell him the story. And then you and I can go look for Mr. Harris."

"I wish we'd take care of Harris first," Clinton said. "Then the rest would be easy."

Pearse agreed. "It would be, but you can bet we'll have a hard time finding Harris if he doesn't want to be found. Do it my way, and he'll come to us."

"Now that that's settled," Molly Thatcher said, "let's have some supper. You folks are probably starving."

Nobody argued with her, and the three trooped out to the back porch to wash up a little before they sat down to a good meal.

The Platte River meanders along the south edge of Julesburg, and in that dry season it was down to a trickle. Clinton took the horses to put up in Colonel's livery stable and fill

Colonel in on the latest developments, and Pearse followed the river into town on foot. While Clinton was making himself to home in the hotel, Pearse would find Carrington and fill him in. He guessed he could sneak over to the north edge of town after that and tell Colonel he was back and that they'd take care of Harris before risking anybody's life.

But on second thought, he guessed he'd stay away from the stable. Colonel could go on worrying a little longer, and it wouldn't do him any harm. Mary Lou would be safe at the ranch, and so long as Harris didn't see any money, so would Colonel.

It was a pretty night with the moon coming out of the first quarter, and Pearse could smell the sage he crushed underfoot, and the clover and tallgrass as well. He watched Clinton out of sight, and then he followed the river.

A couple of times a dog barked at him, but he guessed it wouldn't matter. There was enough noise coming from the town so one or two dogs barking wouldn't be noticed.

There were the usual rinky-tink sounds of a music box trying to hold its own against a piano in each of six different saloons and the general murmur of voices and an occasional raucous yell when somebody had a run of luck bucking the tiger.

He floated along through the distant sounds of Julesburg and the more immediate sounds of frogs and the little wind that came down from the mountains, and he relaxed the way he generally did when he knew he had only a little time to relax before things started to get serious.

He'd had the feeling just before the deal in a poker game, and he'd had it just before a fight. It helped, because it kept you from tensing up too soon and getting tired just when you needed your wits and your strength and your skill the most.

Chaper Twelve

There was a back alley behind the jail, and Pearse followed it until he saw the bars on the windows, and then he squeezed between the jail and the next building and looked out into the street. He had debated between riding up the street to the front door and coming in on foot. Foot won. He didn't need to advertise his presence in town, and even though the jail was probably the last place Harris would think of coming to, somebody else might recognize him and pass the word, and before long all of Julesburg would know that Charlie Pearse was back in town.

There didn't seem to be anybody out on the street this far down, although he could see the yellow lights of the saloons begin a hundred yards to the east. The men who were coming in or going out were busy with their own affairs. Pearse slipped around the corner of the building and tried the front door.

Sheriff Carrington was sitting behind his desk, a worn and cut-down Army Colt and a cup of coffee on the desk beside him. He was looking straight at the door, like a sensible man.

"Come for your letter, Charlie? I didn't hear your horse."

"Didn't ride him. I need to talk to you, Sheriff. I got some trouble, and it looks like I brought it your way."

"Get yourself a cup of coffee and set. Talking's easier when a feller gets comfortable."

Pearse got a cup off the rack and filled it from the pot on the stove, and then he told the sheriff the story as far as it had gone. He even remembered to say that Ellen Murphy had escaped from the Deadwood jail.

"Well, it's quite a tale," Carrington said when he was finished. "Now you got to figure out whether Harris is in town or not. Then you got to get the money out of the bank come morning and deliver it to Reynolds. And after that, you got to pick up the lady out at the ranch and bring her to Colonel. All without Harris knowing about it. Is that it?"

"Well, not quite all. I got to help Marshal Clinton get Harris. He deputized me. Besides, he helped me, so I have to help him."

"Gave your word, did you? Then I guess you got to help. Where's Clinton now?"

"Down to the hotel, I guess. I told him to get himself a room and I'd be along after I talked with you." Pearse remembered something. "One other thing. Colonel doesn't want anybody to know about that money. I don't know why, but that was part of the deal."

Carrington nodded. "Don't make me no never mind. I can keep my mouth shut with the best of them. Just so long as it don't interfere with the law, if you take my meaning."

"I don't think there's anything wrong with the money, if that's what you mean. It's honest, from what I hear. Man won it gambling and made a good investment."

"All right. Now Harris knows you by sight and by name, so you want to stay clear. Is that it?"

Pearse nodded. "I don't think he knows Clinton, but I could be wrong about that."

"He don't know me," Carrington said, but Pearse knew he was thinking that his sheriff's star pointed him out as a potential enemy. "What we ought to do now is go up to the hotel and have a little visit with the marshal and figure out what we're going to do next."

"All right," Pearse agreed. "But we'll go in separately. That way Harris won't tie you to me, in case he's watching."

Carrington went out the front door, Pearse out the back. The stores in the west end of town were closed, but there were lights on in a few of the houses, and the windows were open in most of them because of the heat that lingered from the afternoon.

There were voices in those houses, voices of peaceable folk who were catching up with the doings of the day before they went off to bed. Julesburg had come a long way since George and Charley Bent had burned the town fifteen years before. They and the band of Cheyenne they led had cut the telegraph line and caused stage service to be suspended for six months. But George was an interpreter for the Government now, and Charley was somewhere in the Southwest raising hell.

It was all history now, Charlie Pearse thought, and Julesburg was just another wild frontier town about its business of making money off horse and cattle trading and raising a little hell when it didn't interfere with business.

Pearse went around the south edge of town to get to the hotel. Most of the buildings were stores and were closed, so he had no problem there, but the one next to the hotel, a dry-goods and hardware store, was open, and yellow lamp light spilled out the rear door. There was a little business going on, and two clerks were running around filling orders while the proprietor kept the customer talking.

He stayed at the edge of the light until he figured it was safe, and then he moved across into the dark at the rear of the hotel.

The hotel was home to him now; he had lived there for over a year in a second-floor room. In the back hallway Jesse Spence had been shot by the man they called the Shooter. In the front lobby Sheriff Carrington had posted Pearse that same night to protect Jim Thatcher and his wife. Pearse knew the building the way he knew the High Plains.

He went in the back door and walked carefully up the hall to the door that led to the lobby. The clerk was dozing behind the desk, the register beside him. Pearse knocked gently on the wall, and the clerk turned around. Pearse put his finger to his lips, and the clerk nodded and came back to him.

"Did a man named Clinton register tonight?"

"He's in two-oh-nine. I don't want no trouble, Charlie."

"There won't be any," Pearse assured him. "He's a friend. Has anybody been around asking for me?"

The clerk nodded. "A tall fellow, well-dressed. He said he was a business acquaintance of yours."

"Did he say he'd be back?"

"He just walked out the door, Charlie. You know him?"

"Might could be," Pearse said noncommitaly. But of course he knew him. Gentleman Harris, with his West Point polish and his air of refinement. Harris, with his lack of conscience and his total ruthlessness. A deadly man with a penchant for the good life, and devil take any man who stood in his way. Or woman, for that matter.

And not stupid either. Smart enough to figure out that there would be a back entrance to the hotel, that there would be more than one way of getting into a man's room. Smart enough to know that Pearse had to be kept alive until he figured out where Pearse had the money belonging to Colonel. And then smart enough to kill Pearse when he had it.

Pearse thought about it while the clerk walked back to his desk, and then he went into the lobby after him. "If he calls again, tell him he can probably find me at the Emporium or at Dick Martin's."

"All right, Charlie." He searched the board and handed Pearse his key, and then Pearse climbed the stairs to the second floor and went down the hall to his room. It was across the hall from Clinton's room, and he could have stopped to see Clinton. But then whoever might be in Pearse's room could hear what they had to say. On the other hand, if Harris was waiting in his room, Clinton could hear what Harris had to say.

It worked, to a point. Pearse used the key and walked in as if he didn't have a care in the world, and then he got the big surprise of the day. Harris wasn't there.

"Good evening, Mr. Pearse," Ellen Murphy said. "Do come in. We need to have a visit."

Pearse looked at the tall lady with the nicely-tailored clothes and the cut-down Navy Colt in her hand. "You must have made tracks," he said. "Picked up some new duds too."

"Where there's a will, there's a way," she smiled. "Besides, I had an incentive. Twenty thousand dollars, my friend. I want it."

She was sitting on the edge of the bed where she could move fast, and there was no way Pearse could get to her before she could use the gun. If she had to choose between her freedom and twenty thousand dollars, Pearse knew which way she'd jump.

He walked over to the only chair and sat down. "I don't have it. I figured something like this might come up, and I put it in a safe place until I could be sure you and your friend were out of the game."

"Not likely, Mr. Pearse. Now you're thinking that I won't shoot because you know where the money is and I don't. You're probably right. I'll shoot if you force me, but otherwise we'll just have a nice friendly talk. You start."

"What are we talking about?"

She smiled. "First, let's talk about that U. S. Marshal who had me thrown in jail."

"All right. He got a telegram saying you'd busted out, and then he turned Miss Reilly and me loose to find our own way to Julesburg. He said he was going back up to Deadwood to look for you."

"Very good, Mr. Pearse. Now we'll talk about the money."

Pearse grinned. "That's what it all comes down to, isn't it? I stopped in Laramie and got a letter of credit. I gave it to a friend to hold for me until it was safe."

Ellen Murphy nodded and lowered the gun. Not much, but some. "I have a perfectly good business proposition for you. You pick up the letter of credit, and the two of us will go to the bank and cash it. Then you will walk out with five thousand dollars and tell Mr. Reynolds you were held up along the way and that you have no idea where it is."

"Colonel'd be mighty mad if I came up with that story."

She gave him the smile again. She looked like a puma about to pounce. "That, Mr. Pearse, is your problem."

"I've got a problem for you," Pearse said. "What are you going to do about your friend Harris?"

"What's he got to do with it?"

"He's here in town, and he wants to see me too. Maybe he'll make me a better offer."

"I doubt it. And I can take care of Mr. Harris by myself, thank you."

There was a right time and a wrong time for everything, and Clinton picked the wrong time. He kicked the door open and stood there framed in the light from the hall, so of course Ellen Murphy shot him.

One minute he was standing there saying something like, "You're under arrest," and the next second he was stumbling backward across the hall as if a mule had kicked him. She had hit him somewhere in the torso, and it had doubled him over.

Pearse dove for the floor and grabbed for the Starr at the same time, and a shot whacked the woodwork behind him. He guessed it was maybe to let him know that freedom was a tad more important than money to her.

By the time he had the Starr out and was ready for action, she was gone, running lightly down the hall to the back stairs and freedom. Pearse went out in the hall and bent over Clinton. He was unconscious, but breathing. The ball had gone in under his left upper rib, and it had gone on through to make a hole in the door of two-oh-nine. Pearse holstered the Starr and ripped off the tail of his shirt and wadded it into the holes. The sucking sound from his breathing subsided, and Pearse guessed he might make it, if there was no further damage.

Footsteps pounded up the front stairs, and Pearse turned to face Sheriff Carrington and a deadly-looking sawed-off Greener shotgun. Just to be on the safe side, he put his hands on top of his head.

Carrington snorted. "Who in hell is that?"

"Marshal Clinton. We better get him to the doctor fast, or he won't make it. I think he took one through the lung."

"Did you shoot him?"

"Hell, no," Pearse said. "I got too many enemies right now to go around shooting my friends."

"Where's Mr. Harris?"

"I don't have any idea. It was Ellen Murphy shot him."

A head popped out of a doorway further down the hall, and Carrington motioned to it. "Lend a hand here. We got a badly wounded man we got to get to the doctor."

"I was just . . ."

Carrington motioned to Clinton's body. "Get the feet and don't give me an argument."

Pearse recognized the skinny drummer from the train. The man carefully locked his door, and then he came and took hold of Clinton's feet. "Shouldn't we have something to carry him on?"

Carrington nodded. "Take off a door, Charlie. I'll get a couple more fellers to help."

Pearse used his knife point and the butt of the Starr to knock out the hinge pins from his door and carried it into the hall. They laid Clinton on it, and Pearse adjusted the makeshift bandages again, and then they started for the stairs. The clerk came to lend a hand, and Carrington brought up the rear. "Any chance of catching her, Charlie?"

"Slim to none. She ran down the back stairs."

They carried the marshal down the street to the doctor's office, which was the downstairs part of a little frame house. His wife served as his nurse, and Carrington went on ahead and had the two of them ready for business by the time Pearse and the drummer got there with Clinton. No one else had come to help.

"Bad," the doctor said half-an-hour later. "Lucky it missed the gut. Lucky somebody plugged the holes. If air gets in, there ain't much hope after that."

Carrington nodded, and then he thanked the drummer and motioned for Pearse to help him with the door. They walked back up the street to the hotel and left the door with the clerk.

"We got to talk, Charlie," Carrington said.

Chapter Thirteen

Carrington leaned the Greener in the corner behind his chair and laid his cut-down Colt on top of his desk. "Now," he said. "How did Clinton come to be shot?"

"He made a little mistake," Pearse told him. "I went to my room first, because I wanted to see if Harris was there waiting for me. If he was, I figured Clinton could listen in and then maybe we could take him when he left. But Clinton came charging in and stood in the doorway."

"Did he at least have his gun out?"

Pearse nodded. "I guess he hadn't figured on the woman being there, and when he saw her, he kind of froze."

"And she didn't."

"She didn't. Remember, this is the woman who helped kill an old couple and four outlaws. She looks like a lady, and she acts like a lady, but she's a killer. The only reason she didn't shoot me is because she needs me alive to get the money for her. She even made me a proposition. If I got the money out of the bank, she'd give me five thousand of it."

"Did you believe her?" Carrington smiled.

"The same way I believe in Santa Claus."

"Uh-huh. Charlie, you know the drill. Raise your right hand and repeat after me."

"I'm already deputized as a U. S. Marshal, Sheriff."

"And if Clinton kicks the bucket? That star won't mean a damn thing. Better safe than sorry, Charlie."

The Sheriff read him the oath, and then he fished around in his drawer and found a deputy's badge and handed it to Pearse.

Pearse pinned it to his shirt to replace the Marshal's star. "I guess that means you believe in me."

"It means that whatever hit Clinton, it wasn't that cannon you carry around with you. Besides, while you were going down the front stairs with the clerk and the drummer, I found a man on the first floor who heard the shot and stuck his head out the door in time to see a woman running down the back stairs."

Pearse nodded. "Where do we go from here?"

"First of all, it's me and you. I got two deputies, but they're off chasing a horse thief. They could be gone for a week. Second of all, from what you've told me, Harris and Miss Murphy are apt to shoot each other on sight. That might save us some trouble."

Pearse thought about it. "Ellen Murphy has a big hate for Harris right now, but that wouldn't stop her from teaming up with him until the money shows up. She got her feelings ruffled when he knocked her out and left her to face the music, but she's not the kind of person to let a little thing like feelings stand in the way of money."

Carrington searched in his desk drawer again and came up with a pint of bourbon. He took a healthy swig and passed the bottle. Pearse took a smaller one, just to be sociable.

"Another thing. What happened to the gold from the stage?"

"I don't know," Pearse admitted. "I'd guess that there wasn't as much as they let on, or else Harris wouldn't be in town waiting for me to give him twenty thousand dollars. He would have been satisfied with sixty thousand from the stage, if it had meant his freedom to come after Colonel's money."

"There's never too much money for a thief, Charlie."

"I'll agree, but Harris wants to buy himself some respectability. He's not going to be that kind of thief forever. He's too fancy to take money with a gun if there's another way."

Carrington shrugged. "You know the man, I don't." He looked at the pint again, and then he corked it and put it back in the drawer. "Way I see it, you're going to have to be the bait. Both Harris and the lady know you. Both of them are after you, either together or separately. The only way I can get close to them is to watch you and see who comes after you."

"I have to hand it to you, Sheriff. You come up with some real great ideas."

Carrington ignored the sarcasm. "Glad you see it my way, Charlie. If I was you, I'd go back to the hotel and get cleaned up and ketch some sleep."

Pearse didn't bother telling him that he'd have to put the door back on his room or that there wasn't much chance he'd get any sleep in that room with both Harris and Miss Murphy looking for him. He already knew that, just the way he knew that letting Pearse be the bait was the best way to catch the two of them.

"Where are you going to be?" Pearse asked.

"I'll be looking around town. I'll stop by the hotel every once in a while to check on you."

"I've got a better idea. You go home and get some sleep, and I'll find me a safe place, and then we'll go out together in the morning when we're all rested up."

Eventually Carrington agreed. He pointed to the cells. All three were vacant, and he took one and Pearse took another, and they both got a taste of what it was like to spend a night behind bars.

In the morning they went down to the cafe for a good breakfast of steak and eggs, and then Pearse went to the hotel and changed clothes while Carrington nosed around looking for anyone who had seen Ellen Murphy. Pearse found clean clothes, but Carrington found no one who had seen Ellen Murphy.

It struck Pearse that she had been neatly dressed, not the sort of clothes a woman on the run from the law might be expected to wear. She had made good time getting to Julesburg from Deadwood, she had a place to stay, and she was apparently familiar enough with Julesburg to find her way around without assistance.

When Pearse told that to Carrington, the Sheriff grunted and said that a woman like that had probably found a friend to help her. "She could have come directly here using the stage and the train, the way you did," he reminded Pearse. "She didn't have to stop in Laramie and do any business when her business was all right here."

"Where'd she get the money for the stage?"

"I'd say she found somebody in Deadwood who was willing to stake her. Maybe she took it at gunpoint, Charlie. That ain't important. What is important is that she's here and that she doesn't give a damn who gets killed while she takes care of her business with you."

It wasn't the happiest thought in the world, but it was all Pearse had to work with.

Over a second cup of coffee, Carrington hatched his plan. He and Pearse would go to the bank and take out a canvas sack and give it to Colonel. It might put Colonel on a worse spot than he was on already, but that couldn't be helped. It would at least give him notice that Harris and Murphy were after the money still, and it would let him know that both his intended and his bank roll were safe for now.

Pearse had nothing better to offer, so they walked down to the bank and picked up a canvas sack filled with scrap paper from the trash barrel. The banker didn't crack a smile. He promised not to mention the transaction to anyone, and he assured Carrington that he was ready to do some real business whenever the sheriff was.

"How well do you know Reynolds?" Carrington asked Pearse.

"I've played poker with him, and that's about it. I stable my horse there, and I know some of the men who work for him. They seem to like him well enough. I could probably count on Josh in a pinch."

"Let's get things started then, and after we see Colonel, we'll drop on by the doctor's and see how Clinton's making out."

Colonel was glad to see Pearse. He listened while Pearse told him about Mary Lou and the money, and while Carrington unfolded his plan. He only had one objection: how was he supposed to protect Mary Lou when he was here in town and she was out at the Thatcher ranch?

"I'm just supposed to sit here and do nothing? And Mary Lou's going to wait out there at Thatcher's place? Hell, she needs me!"

"She won't need you for now," Pearse assured him. "Jim Thatcher'll make sure she's safe. Besides, she's out of the way there, and it's not too likely that Harris could trace her to Thatcher's place."

Colonel snorted. "He's apt to do the unexpected. I knew him back at the fort, and he was a cagey, snotty sombitch, if you want my opinion. I never trusted him. He was after anything in skirts, and he broke a few hearts around there before he run off with another officer's wife."

Pearse nodded. "Ellen Murphy, of course. When we caught up with her before, Mary Lou told us something about her."

"That's her. She was the one who was full of grand plans, the way I heard it. First Harris was after Mary Lou, but she wouldn't have anything to do with him. I was a sergeant then, and I didn't figure I had a chance with Mary Lou. But then I got lucky at cards and put some of my extra money with her daddy's commissary. About then he suggested I go shares with him, and then it was all gravy from then on out."

"There's money to be made that way," Carrington said. "If a man's inclined to go into business." Carrington's tone of voice indicated that he wasn't so inclined.

"Charlie," Colonel said. "What did you find out about John Logan?"

Pearse told him what Mary Lou had told him, that Logan had been a bystander at a saloon fight and had caught a stray bullet. "It sounds like an accident to me," he said. "One of those things that happen in a town like Deadwood."

"Yes," Colonel said. "I suppose it figures. John lived a hard life, what with the Indian wars and all. And then he stopped a slug meant for another man."

"Ironic," Pearse said.

"Exactly. I knew John pretty well over the last ten years. He was a good man."

And that was about all the epitaph John Logan would get, Pearse thought. Colonel was not sentimental, and in the life he had led as an Army non-com, death was probably as commonplace as breakfast. Maybe there really was no more to be said.

Carrington cleared his throat. "We'll let you go, then. Right now, me and Charlie are going down to see how the marshal's doing."

Mary Lou was enjoying herself. She helped Molly Thatcher with breakfast, and after Jim rode out to see to the day's work, Molly took her on a tour of the immediate area. They walked down to the bunkhouse and the kitchen, where she met Joe, the Mexican cook. Then they saddled horses and rode through the morning, headed up-valley to where Molly said the shooter had started killing cattle.

"Charlie Pearse took care of that for us," Molly said. "We didn't know who was doing it. We thought it was one of the riders had gone crazy, but it wasn't that at all. It was the foreman, he had some idea he'd kill enough cattle to run Jim into the ground and make him sell for peanuts. I figured in it too. I think his plans included me."

"And Charlie stopped it?"

Molly nodded, and it was easy to see that remembering was a painful business. "Caught the man when he came to kill Jim. Shot him right behind the house."

"I guess he had reason," Mary Lou said. "He's not a back-shooter, Charlie isn't."

"No," Molly agreed. "Charlie Pearse is a good man."

When the sun was almost overhead, they turned back. Mary Lou unsaddled the horses and put them up while Molly went on to the house to start dinner. When Mary Lou was finished, she washed up on the back porch and went inside to help.

"Jim's easy to please," Molly said. "Give him his steak and potatoes, and he'll do you a favor and eat some buttered carrots and butter beans to keep you happy. Add on some cherry cobbler, and he's died and gone to Heaven."

The door opened and the man himself walked in. "Now, that is what I call luck," he said. "I got me two ladies cooking, and ain't that a treat!"

Molly grinned. "See what I told you? The way to a man's heart is through his stomach. Every dang time."

It was good to see two people happy. Mary Lou hoped she and Colonel would get along as well, and then she thought, Of course we will. We know each other about as well as any two people can, and the way he loves me and I love him, it's got to work out just fine.

And then the door opened again, and it all went to hell in a handbasket, as her father used to say.

Harris stood there with a crooked grin on his face and a big Army .45 in his fist. "How bucolic," he said. "I do admire to see happy people."

"Who in hell are you?" Jim Thatcher demanded. "And what's the sixgun for?"

"For whoever's fool enough to try my patience. This lady's going with me for a while. Mary Lou? Tie up this fellow." He tossed her a length of rope. "When you're done, tie up the lady too."

Long ago Pa and Colonel had told her never to argue with a gun that was pointed at you. She grabbed the rope. "You'll never get away with this, Harris. Colonel will have your hide for it."

"Permit me to disagree. You'll keep me company for a while, until Mr. Pearse and I complete a little business transaction, and then you and Colonel can be reunited, so to speak."

"Harris, if I wasn't a lady, I'd tell you you were the meanest, lowdown sombitch alive. You're nothing but a murdering scoundrel and a common thief."

Harris laughed. "Flattery won't work either, Mary Lou. Tie them up good, or I shoot them one by one. It'd be a hell of a lot easier, I assure you. But I'm doing you and them a favor."

There was nothing to do but comply. Even if the cook heard shots, there was probably nothing much he could do against a murderer like Harris. She tied the rope as loosely as she dared in the hope that Jim or Molly would be able to free themselves and come to her rescue, but it was a vain hope at best.

When she was done, Harris had her turn around and stuffed gags in Molly and Jim's mouth. Then he pushed her through the door, and there was no mercy in the noonday sun or in Harris either.

"Where are you taking me?"

But Harris didn't answer. It was as if he considered the question too foolish to deserve an answer. Instead, he pushed her ahead of him back of the house and over a little rise into a stand of pines. There were two horses tethered to one of the pines, and he ordered her to mount one of them.

She vaulted into the saddle and considered kicking the horse into a gallop and riding off, but he was ahead of her there. He left the horse tethered while he tied her feet together under the horse's belly, and then he took a clean handerchief from his pocket.

"Bend down," he ordered. "I'll do the looking for both of us." He tied the handkerchief over her eyes, folding it three times to make sure she couldn't see, and then he mounted the other horse. She heard the creak of the saddle. Then he untied both horses and rode away from the trees, leading her horse.

"You've got nothing to worry about," he said. "We're going to have a little ride, and then I'm going to put you in a nice safe place for a while, until Mr. Pearse and I do our business."

"And then?" she mumbled. He heard her.

"Why, then I'll turn you loose to find your Colonel and go on with your life. One other thing. If you should be foolish and try to escape, I'll be forced to kill you. And I'll make sure to kill Colonel too."

She remembered the elderly couple shot down in their home, and the four outlaws dead around their fire. She knew she could count on Harris to keep his word. Of course he might kill her and Colonel after that, but it was a chance she had to take.

The sun beat down on her head, so she knew it was still early, and then after a while it was hot on her face, so she knew they were headed west. They stopped twice to rest, and Harris loosened the gag to let her drink from a canteen. And then it was cooler and they stopped for a long while. In the distance she could hear the faint sound of pianos and voices, and she knew there was a town nearby. Julesburg? Maybe.

There was nothing to do but wait and see what happened next.

Pearse and the sheriff went down the street to the west, making a perfunctory check of the saloons as they went. Neither of them expected to find Harris waiting for them. He would pick his time and his place, and then he'd move. They didn't expect to find Murphy, either. She'd have holed up for the day long since. When they moved, Pearse thought, it would be after dark when they'd have all the cover they needed.

They covered the north side of the street and then they turned back and covered the south side until they were once again opposite the livery stable.

"Want to go back and check on Clinton?" Pearse suggested.

"Not right away. Let's go see Colonel again."

Colonel put down his pen and marked his place in his account book. "Find anything?"

"Nothing. I figure he'll move after dark," Carrington said.

"I'd be a hell of a lot happier if I were with Mary Lou."

"She's as safe as she can be," Pearse said, and in the next minute he wished he'd kept his mouth shut.

Josh came through the door. "Mr. Reynolds, there's a man here says he's got to see you. He says it's life and death."

And Jim Thatcher walked in.

"Mary Lou's gone," he said. "A man came in the house and took her at gunpoint. He said you can have her back when he and Charlie finish their business."

Colonel's mouth went thin, and then he slammed his fist on the table. "I might have known that no-good bastard would pull something like this."

"Always the unexpected," Carrington said. "Did you happen to see which way they went?"

"No. He tied us up, me and Molly. From the sound of the horses, I'd say to the north. Up the valley. But that could have been a way to put us on a false trail." He turned to Colonel. "Colonel, I can't tell you how sorry I am. I had no choice. From what Charlie and the marshal said, he'd have shot us all, if he'd had to."

"All right, Thatcher. It's done. I couldn't have done any better, if it comes to that. Anybody out looking?"

"I put three men out," Jim Thatcher said. "Jesse out to the north, Hank out to the east, and Honus to the south. I left Joe up at the house in case he comes back. I come in to town, and I figured if he did too, I'd ketch up with him."

"Just to make sure, what did this man look like?" Carrington asked.

"Big, maybe six foot or a tad over. Dressed in a nice black suit. Looked like a lawyer or a preacher. Somebody like that."

It was Harris to a fault. Not that Carrington had expected it to be a flunky. Harris wouldn't trust a job like that to anYbody else.

Carrington nodded. "Figures. We're going to do this all legal and proper. Charlie here is deputized. I want to deputize the two of you, so there's no problem later."

"There won't be any problem if I get my hands on him," Colonel said. "He won't be around to cause one."

Carrington looked at him. "This Harris is a fugitive from justice, and he is to be brought in alive to stand trial for murder. Marshal Clinton wants him for that and for armed robbery, and he's got a warrant out of Deadwood."

"Where is Clinton?" Thatcher asked.

"At Doc's. Ellen Murphy shot him last night."

Jim cleared his throat. "Sheriff, I can spare three men. You want to deputize them?"

"In good time. Colonel, if I'm to deputize you, I want your word that you won't kill the man unless there's no other way."

Colonel pursed his lips. "All right," he said finally. "I guess I don't get to go unless I give my word, huh?"

"You got that right."

"All right. You have my word."

Carrington nodded. "Raise your right hands and repeat after me." Pearse watched as they went through the ritual that transformed them from citizens into temporary lawmen. When Carrington was done and had passed out the tin, he said, "Colonel, I'm going to leave you here in town. You know Harris by sight, and he's going to have to get in touch with you to say where and when he wants the ransom paid. If he shows up, you can arrest him and hold him."

He turned to Pearse and Thatcher. "We're going out to your place, Jim. Maybe we can pick up some tracks. And I want to deputize the men you can spare. We'll look every place we can think of to see if we can find her."

"I could pay the twenty thousand," Colonel said. "If that would bring her back, I'd do it without hesitation."

"It wouldn't," the sheriff said bluntly. "The only reason she'll be alive is if he figures he needs her for bargaining power. Don't count on paying him off at all."

Chapter Fourteen

Pearse and Carrington led the way to the doctor's office. Carrington had borrowed a horse from Colonel, and he went inside while Pearse and Thatcher stayed out with the horses.

"I feel like I let Colonel down pretty hard," Thatcher said.

"You were up against a hard man," Pearse told him. "It could have happened to anybody."

"We were all inside getting ready to eat," he went on, just as if Pearse hadn't spoken. "He just walked in and stood there with a gun. He made Mary Lou tie me and Molly up, and then he held a gun on her and told her she was going with him. She went. What else could she do?"

"Not a thing. And you couldn't either. I know the man, and he'd have killed the three of you if you'd made a play."

Carrington came out. "He's still unconscious. Doc says if he makes it through today, he has a chance. He said the ball got the top of one lung, but he's all right if it don't start to supperate. That's a fancy word for pus, I think."

Thatcher nodded. "What Doc's sayin' is, he's going to get better if he don't die. That's not telling us much, is it now?"

Carrington gave him a wintry smile. "That's Doc for you. Charlie, you got any ideas where she might be?"

"Well, if he kept her alive, he'd want to put her someplace out of the weather. I'd say let's try the line shacks."

"There's two of them, ain't there? One up north in the valley, and one south of the Julesburg trail."

Thatcher nodded. "We can look over the south one when we ride out to the ranch. It's not far off the trail."

Carrington swung into the saddle. "We'll split when we get there. Jim, you and Charlie can check out that south shack, and I'll ride on to the ranch and deputize your men. Then we'll figure out where to go from there."

They rode out of town together, Jim on a fresh horse from Colonel's stable, and after ten miles at a trot, Pearse and Thatcher split off and headed for the line shack.

They came up to it slowly and on foot, Thatcher standing to one side while Pearse kicked the door open. The shack was flimsy, and it shook when Pearse kicked the door. The tarpaper sheathing quivered.

There were no windows, and it was dark even though it was late afternoon outside, but there was enough light coming through the open door for Pearse to see that nobody was inside. It looked pretty much the same as it had last fall: a cast iron stove, some cow chips and kindling for fuel, and a coffee pot and a battered skillet, in case somebody got stranded by weather. There was no fire in the stove and no sign that anybody'd made one recently. There weren't any footprints that he could see, and outside there were no fresh horse tracks. Wherever Mary Lou Reilly had been taken, it wasn't here.

"Looks bad," Thatcher said. "If he kept her alive, he'd want to make sure she was out of the weather."

"Maybe he took her to the north shack," Pearse said, but he really didn't believe it. Harris was too smart to pick an obvious place, especially one that riders would be using from time to time.

They mounted and rode north to the ranch.

But there was no word of her there, either. Hank and Honus had drifted in reporting nothing for five miles up and down the trails. Jesse Pence had gone as far as the north line shack and found nothing.

Pearse and Joe, the cook, circled the ranch buildings and eventually found where Harris had tied his horses. He had ridden in on his own and stolen another from Jim's cavvy. Then he'd ridden off, leading the other horse with Mary Lou on it. First he'd gone north, up the valley, and then he'd cut over a ridge to head west. Then he'd followed the Julesburg trail where the tracks merged with all the others that had passed that day. Harris was nothing if not cagey. "It's kind of annoying, ain't it?" Carrington said. "I don't know what good we're doing."

Hank and Honus were miles behind them, checking the trail in the other direction.

"The way I see it," Pearse said, "Harris has to come to us to get the money. We might as well go back and keep Colonel company and wait for Harris to make his play."

After the sheriff had gone home to a late supper, Pearse put up his horse at the livery stable and walked down the aisle to Colonel's office. Colonel was sitting behind his desk, which was littered with papers. It reminded him that Colonel had other irons in the fire than his livery stable. Pearse guessed that he was quietly buying land around Julesburg. With more ranchers starting to fence in range, it was possible to get into the cattle business without touching a cow: you got the land and rented it out for grazing.

It was a gamble, of course, because a lot of cattlemen didn't hold with fencing; they liked things the way they were, with a free range and no holds barred. But the future was getting to be the present, the way it generally did, and sooner or later, Pearse guessed, they'd have to come to Colonel.

Colonel looked up, a hard look that told Pearse about how he felt. Just in case Pearse missed the point, he said, "I thought you could be trusted, Charlie. Now I've lost my girl and I ain't seen a dime of my money. What in hell goes on?"

"The money's still in the bank, Colonel. I can't help what happened to Mary Lou. I figured she was safe out there, and so did you, as I recollect."

"How did that devil find out she was out at Thatcher's?"

Pearse shrugged. "Somebody talked. Somebody let it slip that Jim and I were friends. I suppose Harris added it up and decided it would be easier to lay his hands on the money by taking Mary Lou than it would be trying to take it off you or me."

Colonel thought about that for a minute. "I suppose he thinks I have the money now?"

"That's what I had in mind. I hope somebody let slip that the sheriff and I went into the bank empty-handed and came out with a canvas sack we brought over here and left."

"You better hope so. Because if they didn't, he'll still be after you."

"I don't care if he is," Pearse told him. "There's one thing I hate to do, and that's nothing. I wish he'd make his move and get it over with."

Pearse went back to the hotel and changed clothes, and then he went down to the cafe for dinner. It was good, but he didn't feel much like eating. He didn't feel much like going to work either, but he went down to Dick Martin's saloon and sat at his usual table, facing the door, and waited for business.

After a while the drummer from the night before strolled in and went to the bar. Two other men came along, cowpokes by the look of them, and they got into a conversation with the drummer.

Pearse shuffled the cards on the table, with the ripping sound a deck makes, and then he shuffled them overhand. He put the deck down then and stacked chips in neat piles, blue and red and white.

One of the cowboys turned to look, and then the three men sauntered over and took chairs.

They wanted stud, five-card stud. Pearse watched the antes and dealt. He wished it had been seven-card, because it was a more exciting game. In five-card, there was only one hole card, and everybody could guess at what everybody else had.

They played for a while, nobody getting rich, nobody getting poor. Pearse bet on a couple of hands he wouldn't have touched on another night, because he didn't want to lose the others by being a tight player. Finally, he got what looked like a winning hand. He had an ace in the hole, a king showing. The next round he drew a jack. Nothing in the other hands was higher than a jack, but there were two of them. That meant that the other jack might be somebody else's hole card. In any case, it was nothing to bet his shirt on. It was good enough to stay, not good enough to raise. One of the cowboys held a pair of sevens, and the drummer had a queen to go with his jack by the fourth card. If he had a ten to go with his nine, he could have a straight.

The cowboy raised on the fifth card. He had another seven showing, and he looked like a sure-fire winner. Pearse didn't raise, even though he had pulled a ten on his fourth card and a king on the fifth. He had a royal straight, but he didn't want to milk the others for all they were worth. It was always better to pass up a little easy money and keep the other players coming back.

The drummer was smarter than he looked. He probably had a straight too, and he hadn't raised.

The cowboy turned his hole card face up and reached for the pot. He had three sevens. The drummer smiled and turned up his hole card. He had a straight to the king.

"Not good enough," Pearse said. He showed them his ace-high straight.

The cowboy took it in good part. He'd overbet a poor hand, and he knew it. You don't go raising on mediocre cards. But the drummer had come close and hadn't made it.

"You never raised," he accused Pearse. "You're supposed to raise."

Pearse shook his head. "I never raise on cards I haven't got. I had nothing at all until the last card."

"Don't be a sore loser, Shorty," the cowboy said. "I bet and I lost. Hell, I even raised, and all you did was stick around."

The drummer wasn't too happy about having his shortcomings as a poker player mentioned, and he tried to get even. "At least I don't go shooting people in the middle of the night."

"I don't either, friend," Pearse told him. "If you're talking about last night, somebody else shot the gentleman."

"Sure," he sneered.

"You're leaving the game, friend," Pearse told him. "You have a big mouth, and there's nothing coming out of it I want to hear."

The drummer picked up cards and started tearing them in half, cursing all the while. The cowboys grinned. It was one way of livening up the evening.

Dick Martin came out from behind the bar and Pearse stood

up. "Game's over for tonight, Dick," Pearse said. "I think the gentleman wants to buy a new deck of cards."

The drummer gave him a killer look, but he fished a dollar out of his pocket to cover the cost of a new deck, and then he went outside with no further fuss.

Pearse bought the cowboys a drink, and then it was time to go, either back to the hotel or down to Doc's to check on Clinton.

The drummer was waiting outside. "I had no call to say that. I apologize."

"Accepted," Pearse said.

"I guess I got pretty hot under the collar."

"It happens."

"It was that woman set me off."

"What woman?"

"The one who shot that fellow in the hall and ran away."

Pearse was suddenly alert. "You saw her? Where?"

"She was back in the hotel tonight. I saw her in the hall on the second floor when I came out."

"Why in hell didn't you say something?" Pearse demanded.

"I was scared," he admitted. "It threw my game way off. I bet everything I had on that hand."

It was a crazy enough excuse to be true, Pearse thought. He handed the drummer a five dollar gold piece and left him. His next stop had to be Doc's, never mind Ellen Murphy.

Doc was awake and so was his wife. "You can't see him, Charlie," Doc said. "I think he's going to make it, but it's touch and go right now, and I don't want him excited."

"All right. If he comes to, tell him that woman's in town. He'll know the one I mean."

"I'll tell him," Doc promised.

"And don't let anybody in to see him except me or Carrington. If that woman finds him, she'll kill him."

"I can handle it," Doc promised. He parted his coat enough for Pearse to see the butt of a pistol stuck in his waistband.

Pearse wondered what Ellen Murphy was doing back at the hotel. For all she knew, she'd killed Clinton. And if she was waiting for Pearse to come back, she could wait a little longer. Colonel ought to know that she was still prowling around.

Down at the livery stable, Colonel was still awake, but just barely. He was dozing over his desk, and Josh and Petey were stretched out on hay bales inside, guarding the doors.

"She's still in town," Pearse said without preamble. "Watch yourself."

"I aim to, Charlie."

"Heard anything from Harris?"

"Nothing. I guess we wait." He yawned. "Maybe I ought to just pay him the damn money when he shows up."

"You do, and Mary Lou's dead. He'll kill her as soon as he gets his hands on the money."

"I've thought of that. But maybe he won't. Maybe he'll take the money and head on out."

"Listen to me, Colonel. He's not going to leave a witness behind to put the finger on him. He's going to kill her. The only reason she may still be alive is because he might need her to get you to turn over the money."

He nodded. "You're right, of course. But it's taking so damn long."

Pearse could have told him that that was part of the game, that Harris was going to keep him sweating as long as he could, because when the showdown came, Colonel would be mentally exhausted and wouldn't know what he was doing. But he didn't. There was just so much one man could take, and Colonel had reached his breaking point.

Pearse was close to it himself, and knowing that Ellen and her gun were out there somewhere didn't make it any easier.

It was a quiet night for Julesburg. Pay day was a week away, and in the middle of the week there wasn't too much doing at any time. A couple of pianos were rattling away in the saloons, and the Crib Row probably wasn't hurting for lack of business, but there were no raucous yells in the middle of the main drag, not to mention the free-for-alls that livened up the evening on a weekend.

Pearse went back to the hotel, sneaking in the back way instead of going through the lobby. There was no sense in letting the lethal Miss Murphy know he was there. Or Harris either, for that matter.

He got one foot on the stairs, and then he heard a voice raised in surprise. He stopped. It might have been nothing, but he didn't want to take the chance.

Something went thump on the floor above, and then there was silence. Pearse slid the Starr out of his holster and waited, flattening himself against the wall. In a moment Harris appeared at the top of the stairs. He was neatly dressed, and his hands were empty.

Pearse raised the Starr and called up to him. "You're under arrest, Harris! Don't move!"

He reacted quicker than Pearse had thought he could. He simply jumped down the stairs, knocking Pearse out of the way and kicking at his gun hand as he came. Pearse cursed and reached for the gun that had fallen to the floor, but by that time Harris was lost in the darkness, and in a moment a horse's hooves beat a tattoo down the alley behind the hotel.

There was no sense in going upstairs, but Pearse went anyway. He had his gun ready when he got to the door of his room, but there was no need for it. Ellen Murphy wasn't going to bother him at all. In fact, she wasn't going to bother anybody again. Harris had hit her hard on the side of the neck, and maybe it was harder than he had wanted to, but the fact remained that she was dead.

Pearse bent over her to make sure, and when he felt for the jugular, there was no pulse. Her head flopped loosely, the way they do when the neck has been broken.

His hand still hurt from the kick, but he was able to hold the gun. He holstered it and backed out of the room, closing the door behind him, and then he walked through the hall to the stairs that led to the lobby, and so out into the street.

Chapter Fifteen

Sheriff Carrington went back to the hotel with Pearse. On the way they stopped at the doctor's, and he promised to come as soon as he got his clothes on.

When the doctor came, he told them what they already knew, that Ellen Murphy had died of a broken neck. It was a good indication of what Harris was capable of.

"You only got one of them to worry about now, Charlie," Carrington said. He had looked at Pearse's hand and decided that he still hadn't killed anybody. "You better watch yourself. That man's fast. Maybe he's faster than you with a gun too."

Pearse nodded. Harris had reacted correctly, and faster than Pearse could have believed. If he'd turned around and run for the front stairs, Pearse would have been behind him with a gun. Even if he'd waited in the hall, he'd have had to shoot Pearse, and that would have killed any chance he had of laying hands on the money.

The undertaker came for the body, and Pearse moved his clothes and the four or five books he owned down the hall to another room. His own was getting too popular with the wrong people.

When Pearse got up the next morning, he went down to the doctor's to check on Clinton. The marshal was sitting up in bed, but he was pale, and he looked like he'd been rode hard and put away wet. "Hear you lost Mary Lou," he said with difficulty.

"Not yet. He's going to have to come up with some kind of ransom note, though. He wants that money too bad to leave it alone."

"Any idea where Mary Lou is?"

"None at all. We looked in all the usual places, the line shacks and the creeks and the caves, and we came up empty."

"Look around town then. He's had time enough to bring her here." And then he suddenly began to cough.

Pearse nodded and started out the door. Doc gave him a dirty look when he came out. "I was just about to remind you that we've got a very sick man in there, Charlie. He don't have no business getting all upset about something he can't help or do anything about."

Carrington was waiting for him outside, and when Pearse told him about Clinton's suggestion that they start looking in town, he agreed. "Seems like that's the way to go. We tried every place outside of town that I could think of, and if she's alive, she's probably here somewheres. Even Harris wouldn't stake her out for the ants."

"I wouldn't bet on it," Pearse said.

"Let's get on down to the livery stable and see what Colonel's got to say."

Colonel had plenty to say. He'd gotten up to find a letter stuck on a stick in front of the door that led to the street. Petey had been asleep and hadn't even known it was there. The note read: "Bring money to the line shack north of the ranch. When I count it, I'll tell you where the girl is."

Harris wasn't giving away any advantages, as Carrington was quick to point out. If Harris told them where Mary Lou was, she might or might not be there. If she was there, she might or might not be alive. Meanwhile, Harris would be free to ride off with the money, and he'd have a good head start on a posse.

Even five years ago, it would have been a lot simpler, Pearse thought. The railroad had made the difference. They could still track Harris while he was on a horse, but he'd probably ride to the nearest railroad and board a train. After that, he'd be gone. Carrington and Clinton would send out telegrams in all directions, but there were too many places a man on the run could hide, and Harris was an expert at hiding.

Colonel scratched a day-old growth of beard. "What do you say we do, Sheriff?"

Carrington rubbed his eyes. He was suffering from lack of sleep the way the rest of them were. "Only one thing to do, Colonel. We'll get the money and take it on out there. I'd say we've got a chance of catching him if we circle the place and get in behind him. I can take a couple of Thatcher's men and do that. You and Charlie will have the money, and you can come in where he can see you. Let him count the money if he wants, and then you can get the information as to where he's got the girl. After that, we'll take him."

Pearse saw one thing wrong with the plan. Harris hadn't said when they were to bring the money. That meant he wanted them to sit out there by the line shack roasting in the sun until they were tired. When he was good and ready, he'd show himself, and not a minute before.

But there was no other way to do it. They rode out to the ranch separately. They stayed long enough to have a cup of coffee and go over the plan. And then they headed out singly, keeping to the high ground. All except Colonel and Pearse, because they wanted Harris to see them.

The first thing they did was go to the line shack and knock on the door. Of course there was nobody there. Harris was too smart to let himself be trapped in a dugout. He needed to be free to move.

"Let's move out a little and see what happens," Colonel said after he'd sniffed around the line shack and satisfied himself that Harris hadn't been there.

"Where do you want to go?"

There was plenty of grass in the valley, but few hiding places. The cattle had been driven north to the high slopes where the grazing would be ideal in summer. There was water higher up, too, the tanks from springs in the rocks were generally full even in the hottest summer. A man couldn't even walk into a herd and hope to hide himself.

"How about those rocks down in the middle? We can leave the horses here and walk down."

"That's kind of obvious," Pearse objected.

"If we're there, he can't sneak up on us from the rear."

"He'll shoot the horses, Colonel. He won't want us trailing him."

"He'll shoot them no matter what, won't he?"

Colonel had the last word, and they walked down the slope to the rocks, which Pearse didn't like at all, because it was low ground and Harris would be on the high ground where he could see every move they made.

The rocks were already occupied by a nest of rattlesnakes, and they whirred and buzzed as Colonel and Pearse approached. Some of them were pretty big, four or five feet long and as thick as a man's arm.

Pearse and Colonel went off to the side a safe distance, and then they squatted on the ground and waited.

There were grasshoppers a-plenty, and the sun burned down out of a pale sky with almost no color. The only thing that made it tolerable was a little wind coming from the head of the valley, twenty miles to the north. Pearse watched the area to the north, Colonel watched the area to the south.

And nothing moved.

The sack of money sat between them in plain sight, like an overgrown toad. If Harris had field glasses, he'd be able to see it and know enough to come in and palaver.

Of course Harris might come in from the east, and then Carrington and Jim Thatcher would pick him up. But Pearse realized that that was wishful thinking. If Harris was as smart as he seemed to be, he'd have been out in the vicinity before daybreak, watching the line shack, noting who was coming and where they had positioned themselves. And if he was extra-smart, he wouldn't be there at all. He'd let Colonel wait out the day in the hot sun, and then he'd come in the evening, when things had cooled down, and he'd make his move.

The sun went down quickly, the way it does when you're in a valley. One minute it was there, and the next there was only bright sky in the west and deep shadow in the valley. There was nothing but black night until the moon came up.

They were tired and thirsty, and the canteens were empty. Harris was probably out there somewhere, but if nobody had been able to spot him during the day, there was little chance of doing it at night.

"Let's call it a day," Colonel said finally, and his voice was the voice of an old man. "He's not going to show."

"I wouldn't bet on it," Pearse said. "Let's wait for moon-rise and see."

And then they heard a horse coming down into the valley from the east. Pearse thought about Mary Lou, where she was and how she was. She had plenty of sand, he thought. If anybody could go through this ordeal, she'd be the one.

Both men had their guns in their lap, and Pearse hoped it would be Harris come to dicker, but then he made out Thatcher's wiry figure and Carrington's dumpy one.

"He ain't coming," Carrington said. "Might as well pack it in and try again in the morning."

Pearse thought about it, and the idea was tempting. Ride back to the ranch and bed down for the night. Drink a gallon of water, cold from the well. Eat a good meal.

"No," Colonel said. "He's watching to see what we're going to do, and when he sees us going back to the ranch, he'll know we set a trap for him."

"Can't let go of it now," Pearse agreed. "If he comes and nobody's here, we'll have the whole thing to do over."

"All right," Carrington said. "We'll leave one of you here to watch for him, and the rest of us can go back. When we've all rested up a little, we'll send another man to relieve the one who's been out here. That way, at least two of us can get some sleep."

"I'll stay," Colonel said. "I'm the one he's looking for."

Carrington and Thatcher had refilled their canteens at the spring near the line shack, and they left them with Colonel. Pearse took a long drink from one of them, and then they were ready to go.

Pearse swung up behind Thatcher, and they rode off across the valley to pick up Pearse's horse. They left Colonel's horse picketed near the spring, where there was water in a little tank dug to catch the overflow, and grass for the taking.

Pearse mounted and followed Thatcher and Carrington across the valley to the west, where they took the high ground.

They followed it for maybe five miles, and then they rode down into the basin at the lower end of the valley.

It had all been for nothing, Pearse thought. The long day in the sun with no protection, the thirst, the heat. The nearness of the snakes in the rocks. And they had wound up with exactly what Harris had wanted in the first place: one man alone with the money.

"I'm going back," he told Carrington. "Colonel's only one man out there, and he could need help before he's done."

"Don't be a fool, Charlie. Harris ain't going to come until tomorrow, when he can see what he's up against."

"All right, I'm a fool," Pearse told him, and then he turned back up-valley.

He had never made the error of thinking of himself as a brave man. He had run as fast as anybody else when trouble showed up that he wasn't sure he could handle. But Colonel had showed himself to be a decent man, and he deserved to have the odds with him. And the pretty girl who had risked her neck to be with the man she loved, she deserved their best effort too.

He got across the valley before the moon was up, which was a point in his favor. He didn't want Harris to see any more than he had to, just in case he was watching. About four miles south of the line shack, he headed up to the top of the ridge and followed that until he was near the shack, and then he turned east to get off the ridge and led his horse the rest of the way.

He took advantage of the spring and drank deeply and filled his canteen. Then he splashed water over his face to take out some of the sting of the heat. And then he picketed his horse alongside Colonel's, where it could drink from the tank.

The moon was up now, a half-moon that bathed the valley in light. Pearse could see the rocks pretty clearly, and he guessed Colonel would be lying in the grass to the south of them. He hoped Colonel would recognize him when he came down there.

At the line shack, he stopped to listen. There was no sound of breathing, no rustle of cloth or squeak of leather that a man might make as he shifted position. Besides, Harris was too smart to let himself get trapped in a dugout where he couldn't see anything except through the doorway.

Nothing moved in the valley either, so he started down the slope toward the rocks and the snakes and Colonel.

He was lying in the grass as Pearse had figured, but he didn't move. Pearse bent down beside him and listened for breathing. It was faint and labored, and when Pearse felt his head, he found a goose egg. He'd been clubbed with a gun butt, most likely.

The money bag was gone.

Chapter Sixteen

"You're covered, Mr. Pearse. Take off your gunbelt. Slow."

He had been lying in the grass a short distance away, and now Pearse could see him crouched and waiting, a Springfield carbine aimed at Pearse's midriff.

Pearse unbuckled his belt and let it slide to the ground. There was never any sense in going for a gun that was already pointed at you. Only a greenhorn could miss at that distance, and Harris was no greenhorn.

"That's fine," Harris said. "Now, where's the money you were supposed to bring?"

"Ask him. He's the one who had it."

"You're lying. If he'd had it, I wouldn't be here."

"No lie. I gave it to him myself."

Harris strolled closer. "You could get to be dead."

"Not until you have the money. You have to make sure you have it in your hand before you kill anybody, don't you?"

It was a nice, normal conversation except that Pearse was scared stiff and he had a .45-70 carbine pointed at him that could blow a fist-sized hole through him.

The argument had some sense to it. If Harris had found the money, Colonel would be dead and Harris would be long gone. What had Colonel done with the money before he was slugged?

"He didn't have a chance to hide it," Harris said in his cultured voice. "He didn't see me coming."

That much Pearse could believe. If Colonel had seen Harris, he wouldn't have stayed still and let Harris knock him out with a blow to the head. He'd have given Harris some punishment, and none showed. Therefore, he'd gotten rid of the money before Harris came up.

"Well? Cat got your tongue?"

"Just thinking. I don't know what Colonel did with the money. He had it with him when I left him."

"There's ways to make you talk," Harris said. It was as if they were in somebody's parlor discussing the weather or the merits of a horse, and that was maybe the key to Harris. He was as cold as a Montana winter. Nothing fazed him. Nothing touched him at all.

"I'd guess you'd know all about that kind of thing," Pearse said. "You learn on Indians? Or did you only torture your own men?"

Harris smiled, and his teeth were white and even in the moonlight. "I don't get angry, Pearse. You might as well stop baiting me and see if you can't remember where the money is."

"I'm not even going to guess. You want the money, go find it."

Harris lunged forward and swung the carbine hard enough to take Pearse's head off, if he'd stood still. Pearse didn't. He fell backward and rolled, and when Harris came in again, Pearse bent his legs and kicked Harris in the gut as hard as he could. Harris backed up and swung the carbine to point it at Pearse, but Pearse rolled again and somersaulted to his feet.

"Want to dance again?"

"You forget. I still have the gun."

"No," Pearse said. "You're the one who's forgetting. You have to have the money in your hand before you kill me."

"Don't bet your last dollar on it. I still have your friend to talk to."

Harris hadn't yelled, but Pearse could hear his breath coming in and out like a steam engine. He'd hurt the man, but not enough. Harris might get tired of fooling around and shoot him for the fun of it. Like he said, he still had Colonel to play with.

"Why don't we talk like a couple of sensible men?" Pearse asked. "For instance, where's Mary Lou Reilly?"

"Money talks louder. Tell me where the money is, and then I'll tell you where the lady is."

"I honestly don't know where the money is, Harris. Tell me where you put the girl, and I'll help you find the money."

Harris smiled, and then he lunged forward with the carbine, hoping to catch Pearse in the midriff. But Pearse saw it coming. He sidestepped and grabbed the barrel to point it away from his body, and then he yanked at it sharply. As he had hoped, Harris had his finger on the trigger, and the carbine boomed in the still night. The barrel burned his hand, but he held on to the weapon and swung it at Harris's head while he was picking himself up. He missed the head but got a shoulder in time to keep him from going for a handgun.

His foot touched something long and coiled, and for a moment he thought he'd stepped on a snake, but it was his gunbelt. He threw the empty carbine at Harris and grabbed the Starr.

"Drop it, Harris. You're under arrest."

Harris laughed. "Table's turned, Pearse. You can't kill me until you find out where the girl is. Think, man!"

"Mexican standoff?"

"That's the name of the game, Pearse."

"I can't afford to shoot you, and you can't afford to shoot me, is that it?"

"That's right. You say you don't have the money. I believe that for now. But we're going to get the money before I tell you."

Pearse thought for a moment, and then he found an ace in the hole. "The money's the least of your worries, Harris. There's warrants out against you in Deadwood and in Julesburg. Tell me where you put Mary Lou, and I'll give you a horse and six hours' start."

"I could work on your friend here," Harris said. "I don't have to deal with you." He grinned provocatively, and Pearse wondered what he was up to now.

Harris motioned with his head, and Pearse followed the motion. In the next moment, Harris was on him like a tiger. Pearse dropped the Starr and jumped to one side, trying to spin the way he had the night he took Billy Kenyon in Dick Martin's saloon. It might have worked on Billy, but it didn't on Harris.

Harris spun right along with him and threw a right at Pearse's middle. It missed and got a rib in passing, and it hurt Pearse. He went backward a couple of feet, but when Harris came in again, Pearse ducked his head and rammed him in the belly. Harris tried to grapple with him, but Pearse wasn't having any. Harris had six inches on him and maybe thirty pounds, and there was no way Pearse could survive a bear hug.

Harris followed him, pushing it for all it was worth, and the next time he threw a right, Pearse jumped to the other side and pushed him off balance. He fell on his right side, and Pearse kicked him in the short ribs and left him out of wind and gasping for air.

Pearse backed off and picked up his Starr and the carbine. The carbine didn't bother him: it was a single-shot and it hadn't been reloaded. Maybe he had a deringer on him, but Pearse wasn't fool enough to get close enough to him to find out.

There was only one thing to do, and he did it. "Get up," he said. "I'm not going to shoot you."

Harris rolled over and got some leverage with his elbow, and when he had raised his head high enough, Pearse hit him on the chin as hard as he could. Harris went out like a light. Pearse watched him for a bit to see if he was faking, and then he rolled him on his belly and buckled his belt around his body and his arms as tightly as he could.

And then he sat down to catch his breath and wait.

He didn't have to wait very long. He and Harris had been fighting for close to an hour, fighting or talking, and pretty soon he heard a horse coming along in the middle of the valley, just as if there was no further need to be careful.

The sheriff looked over the scene of battle. "Had yourself a time, hey? I take it this is Mr. Harris. Where's Colonel?"

Pearse told him. Halfway through the story, Colonel came back to the world, shook his head, and decided it was still there. "Where's he at? I want to get that bastard, if it's the last thing I do."

"You ain't getting nobody," the sheriff said. "In case you forgot, you're a deputy. All we are going to do is take this man back to jail and hold him for the marshal, if he ever recovers. If he don't, we'll get somebody down from Deadwood to take charge of him."

"Where's Mary Lou?" Colonel demanded. "I want to know where my girl is at."

"He never said," Pearse told him. "You still got the money?"

"In a safe place, Charlie. Safest bank I know."

Pearse followed his arm. He had apparently tossed the money bag in the rocks, not knowing that Harris would come or if he came would be able to overpower him, but playing it close to his vest and safe.

"How're you going to get it?" Pearse asked.

"Rope," Colonel said tersely. "I ain't about to walk in there with all them snakes."

Carrington loosened a rope from his saddle and gave it to Colonel. Colonel made a loop and flipped it around the sack. The snakes rattled and hissed at the rope, maybe figuring it was some new kind of snake moving into their territory, but Colonel got the money bag out on the second try.

Pearse used the time to search Harris thoroughly and found a deringer in his left boot. Back where Harris had been lying in wait, he found the Army .45 Harris carried. He guessed that accounted for all the guns.

They tied Harris's legs, and then Carrington rode up to the spring to get the other horses. He had Harris's as well; it had been tied to a shrub a hundred yards from the spring, where he had hoped they wouldn't see it.

Carrington and Pearse hoisted Harris to his saddle, and then they tied his legs together under the horse and ran the rest of the rope around his body and the saddle horn, so he wouldn't fall off. Colonel managed to get to his horse and mount, but he was still very shaky. Pearse wondered if they shouldn't tie him on as well, but Colonel shook his head gingerly. "I got more sand in me than that."

And then they set out for Julesburg by way of the ranch to let Jim Thatcher know that they wouldn't be needing him any more.

Pearse had no great faith in jails, having seen prisoners get out of them without too much trouble, but the Julesburg jail was pretty fair. It had log walls pegged together, and the windows were set with bars let into the logs a good six inches. The door was real iron with a judas window, and it was secured with a hasp and a big padlock that looked like it could have come over with the Mayflower.

Carrington left a deputy in charge, and then they walked down to Doc's office to tell Clinton the good news. Clinton was sitting up, which was a big improvement, and he was even complaining that Doc's wife wouldn't let him eat anything but beef broth or drink anything but milk.

"You lost a lot of blood," Carrington said. "You got to build yourself up before you start getting rambunctious again."

"I feel too good to be eating pap," Clinton snapped. "A good beef steak would do me more good than a gallon of that soup. Hell, it tastes like stale dishwater."

Pearse decided Clinton would be out of bed and prancing around in a week at the most. He might have to keep his chest tied up, but his lungs would be working. That didn't mean he would be in any shape to transport a prisoner to Deadwood, but Pearse guessed Carrington wouldn't be in any hurry to let go of a prisoner facing a murder charge right here in Julesburg.

They left then, Carrington and Colonel to go to their respective homes, and Pearse to go to his hotel room. There would be time to question Harris in the morning.

The moon was going down, a pale shadow of itself in the early morning sky. The breeze from the far-away Rockies was cool and refreshing, and Pearse tried to forget the brutal heat of the day past and the long wait in the sun. But when he lay down at last, he could still hear the whir of insects in the grass and the faint scraping as the nearby snakes rasped over the rocks.

Pearse didn't wake until ten, and then it was only because somebody was pounding on his door. He told them to wait and pulled on his pants, and then he opened the door to the sheriff.

"Get some clothes on and come with me," he said. "Harris got loose."

So it was all for nothing, Pearse thought, the long wait in the sun, the frantic riding here and there, the fighting. Harris was loose.

"What happened?"

"He hung his belt around one of the window bars and around his neck, and then he started making noises like he was strangling. The deputy opened the door and went in to cut him down."

"And then Harris kicked him, took his keys, and locked him in his cell."

"He didn't have to, Charlie. He broke the man's neck. He took a Winchester and a sixgun, and he's got plenty of ammunition for both."

Pearse stared his horror. "The man's kill crazy."

"You could call it that. I sent a boy down to the livery stable to warn Colonel, and I stopped by Doc's to warn Clinton. I figured me and you could go look for him."

"That's about what's left. The two of us."

Carrington shifted his weight, came in the room and sat on the edge of the bed. "Of course we don't know where the girl is. We don't know if Colonel put his money in the bank like a sensible man. But outside of that, everything's just fine and dandy."

Pearse checked his Starr and holstered it. Then he grabbed up the Sharps. "I'm ready. Where do we start looking?"

"I'd say we'll check the saloons and the sporting houses. When we get done, we'll stop by and get Colonel to help us."

Pearse stared at him. "What are we going to do when we find him? Always assuming he hasn't hid out on a boxcar so's he can ride out of town on the train?"

"Follow the law, Charlie. We take him prisoner if we can. If we can't, shoot to kill. I ain't wasting any more lives on Mr. Harris."

Chapter Seventeen

Mary Lou Reilly guessed at the time. It would be about time for breakfast, she thought, because she had had supper and she was getting hungry again.

It was hard to tell the time though, because it was dark. It was dark all the time, because she was in a cellar. It was small, and there were shelves on one wall, so it had to be a root cellar. She had watched carefully when they opened the trapdoor to bring her food and take out the slop bucket, and she was pretty sure that's where she was.

Harris had stopped short of town and come up with a rag and a bottle of something. She was pretty sure that it was chloroform, because it was sweetish to smell and for a couple of hours after she'd come out of it she had a headache.

She knew something else, too. When they came down to feed her and take care of the slop bucket, it was always a woman and never the same one. And they were all dressed fancy, so that meant they were whores and she was in the cellar of a whorehouse.

They untied her hands so she could eat, but they never left her alone. Even when she needed the slop bucket. They stood by and never said a word, no matter how often she asked them how long she was going to be cooped up here.

Life was exciting while she was free, but now she was worried. She might never make it out of here alive.

And wasn't that a morbid thought to be thinking? Maybe it had to do with where she was, in a little hole in the ground. It was really nothing like a grave, though. The one wall had shelves to hold canned goods and such, although there were none there now. And the other three were hard as rock from having been dug out a while ago. You could still see the marks of the spades that had carved the hole out of the earth, but they were dried and hard.

Pa had told her once that there were bad houses in big towns that catered to the needs of men, and that she should be careful never to go near one, because they liked to catch pretty young girls and keep them there forever.

She wondered what Pa would make of all this.

When she thought about it, she realized that a house like this with good-looking women dressed in pretty dresses had to be in a big town, and that meant Julesburg. Lieutenant Harris would be holding her for ransom, and that meant he had to be close to Colonel to be able to produce her when the time was right.

And wasn't that the funny thing? Here she was, probably ten minutes walk from where Colonel was, and he didn't have any idea that she was so close.

And there was no way she could see to get out of this pickle. She hadn't been wearing the belt with the gun and the knife when Harris took her, and that meant she had nothing to work with, even if her hands had been free.

There was nothing to do but wait for Colonel to find her. She tried to think of what people did in books she'd read, but she couldn't come up with anything useful. Mr. Dickens wrote some good stories, but she couldn't recollect a one where somebody was buried in a root cellar.

The closest she could come was that one by Mr. Mark Twain where Tom Sawyer and Becky Thatcher—and wasn't that funny to think of? The same name as Jim and Molly!—had been down in the cave with only a stub of candle to see by. But Becky had had Tom to keep her company, and poor Mary Lou Reilly had no one.

Except for God, of course. But she didn't know what he'd be doing in a bad house, and certainly not in a root cellar. Still, the

Lord worked in mysterious ways, his wonders to perform. There was nothing to do but wait.

And so she waited.

Pearse and the sheriff went together. Pearse had suggested that he take one side of the street and Carrington the other, but Carrington was playing it safe. "If we find him, he's going to shoot first and ask questions after. Even if he gets one of us, the other one can get him."

At each stop they told the bartender who they were looking for and why, and they asked each of them to get word to the sheriff if Harris showed up. It all took a while, because there were twenty-one saloons up and down the street.

Finally they came to the end of them, and they went down to the livery stable to talk to Colonel.

Colonel had a white bandage around his head, and he said it hurt when he moved it, but he didn't think it had addled his brains or anything like that. He listened to Carrington's account of their doings, and then he came up with a suggestion.

"One, I know you have to find Harris. But maybe we ought to be looking for Mary Lou. If we found her, we'd have Harris back where we wanted him. We'd have her and we'd have the money, and he'd have to come to us."

"No," Carrington said. "We had it right the first time around. Get Harris and he'll have to tell us where the girl is."

"And why should he do that?"

Carrington frowned. "Goes against my grain, but I could promise him he wouldn't be charged with killing my jailer and the Murphy woman."

"Could you do that?" Colonel asked.

"Not legally. But then, I wouldn't have to keep my promise, would I?"

Colonel thought about it. "I don't know which I'd want more," he said. "To get that bastard and watch him hang, or to let him get two steps out the door and beat the stuffing out of him. I really don't know."

"But we have to find Mary Lou," Pearse said. "God knows what he's done with her."

Colonel scratched the stubble on his face. "There's one thing I hadn't thought of before. He used to know a madam up at Fort Pierre, and she's in business right here in town. Fat Gertie. You know her place?"

Carington nodded. "A good respectable whore house."

"Well, why not go have a visit with Gertie? If Harris isn't there, she might know where to find him."

"Maybe," Carrington said. "It's worth a try."

It was a brothel like many others. Fairly clean, catering to a more fastidious clientele than most, decorated in the latest style. Pearse thought it would be just the ticket for a cowman with some money in his pocket. He'd be overwhelmed by the surroundings and the lavish attention paid to him, and he wouldn't realize he was being charged double until after it was all over and he had time to think about it.

"Gertie goes back a ways," Colonel said as they walked down the street. "When I was a sergeant out at the fort, Gertie had a hog ranch about five miles out."

Pearse grinned. He knew all about hog ranches. A couple of girls, a couple of beds, and a bouncer, just in case anybody got out of line. All pretty primitive. Not that he'd ever patronized one, but he know about them all the same.

"Gertie came up in this world," Colonel went on. "When they ran her off from the fort area, she came on down here and set up shop. Word around the fort was, she knew Harris and he staked her for a piece of the profits. There is nothing too dirty for the lieutenant to get his paws into."

"That would be a good place to hide a girl," Pearse thought aloud. "Who'd go looking for a nice girl in a cat house?"

Carrington smiled. "Sometimes you ain't as dumb as you look, Charlie."

The sheriff said he'd go to the front door and ask questions. "Charlie, you stay at the back door and stop anybody tries to come out. When me and Colonel get done in the house, we'll come help you search the outhouse and the shed."

Colonel objected. "Gertie knows me, and there's nothing she'd like better than to lead me into a trap. I was the one complained about her to the company commander."

"All right. You take the back and me and Charlie'll go through the house. Remember, when we get done, we'll come out the side door. If one of the girls tries to come through that back door, shoo her back in. If Harris comes through it, take him alive or dead. But if it's dead, you better have a good reason for it."

"Don't worry," Colonel promised. "I'd rather see the sombitch hanged than shot."

Carrington gave Colonel plenty of time to get around back-through the alley, and then he and Pearse went in.

Gertie was not only fat, Pearse thought. She was monstrous. She wasn't a tall woman, maybe five-one or five-two, but she-must have weighed in at two-fifty. She had an orange wig and plenty of paint on her face to fill in the wrinkles. Her eyes were half-hidden by flesh, and lip rouge had rearranged a normally thin mouth.

"Well, ain't you the handsome dudes!" she greeted them. "I can find a couple of ladies would just love to entertain you."

"This is business, Gertie," Carrington told her. "We're looking for a man name of Harris. I understand you used to know him."

"Yes, indeed." Score one for Gertie, Pearse thought. She knew better than to deny it. "A fine figure of a man. But I ain't seen him since the old days up at the fort."

"Call your girls down," Carrington ordered. "Maybe one of them knows something about him."

"Why, no trouble at all, Sheriff." She pursed her mouth, cracking the lip rouge, and gave three piercing whistles. In a moment five young women came down the stairs, smiling and trying to look inviting when they saw the two men.

"All right, Charlie. You stay here and watch them. I'm going to look around upstairs."

"You need a warrant for that, Sheriff," Gertie objected. "You know the law same as I do."

"I got the law," Carrington said, patting his gun butt. "Right here."

He mounted the stairs, slowly, one at a time, wagging his head from side to side. Then he disappeared from view. They listened to his footsteps on the floor above, to the banging of suddenly opened doors, to the sudden silence when he listened for the breathing, the rasp of leather on wood, the hiss of cloth rubbing against itself that would betray the presence of someone.

He took a long time. There couldn't have been more than four or five rooms upstairs. Some of them might have had closets, but Pearse guessed that more than likely a corner had been screened off with a sheet and a wire stretched to hang clothes on. Fancy didn't go much further than the parlor in these houses.

Fat Gertie used her time talking around Pearse to the girls. She told them what a nuisance it was, having that potato of a sheriff poking around in things that didn't concern him. She told them that he was so short of being a man that he had to bring a bumpkin with him to hold his hand.

The girls giggled obediently. One of them had a book in her hand. Another had a piece of paper on which she was writing something. Fat Gertie was too busy talking to notice.

Pearse let the insults roll off his back. When somebody like Fat Gertie insulted you, it was just about the same as a compliment from somebody else. From time to time she gave a glance in Pearse's direction to see how he was taking it, but he just smiled at her. The old country boy grin got you out of more trouble than you could shake a stick at.

"Find anything interesting, Sheriff?" Fat Gertie asked. "Like ladies underwear? Or girdles? Or rouge pots?"

"Not a thing, Gertie," Carrinton grinned. "Unless you count in the fifty dollars somebody was holding out on you."

"What room was that in?" she demanded. "I want to know!"

"I disremember. You better keep wanting."

The girl who had been writing folded the paper small and raised her eyebrow at Pearse when Gertie's back was turned. He had sense enough not to acknowledge the signal.

"If that's all, Sheriff?"

Carrington shook his head. "I'd like all you ladies to go upstairs while we look around down here."

"The hell I will!" Gertie exploded.

"Hell you won't. We've maybe got a desperate man hiding somewhere, and he won't think twice about shooting. I don't want nobody hurt."

Even Gertie was somewhat subdued by that. Pearse moved so he could be next to the door when they headed for the stairs. Gertie led the way, and she started to huff and puff after the first couple of stairs.

The girl who had been writing brushed against Pearse, and he felt her hand slip into his pocket and then dart out again.

They waited until the last of them had disappeared, and then Pearse took the slip of paper out, read it, and showed it to Carrington.

She had written, "Look in the celer."

Carrington opened his mouth and Pearse shushed him. This was something he didn't want Gertie to hear. The less she knew of what was going on, the better off they were.

They went through the parlor, looking behind the sofa, the horsehair chairs, the heavy draperies. Then they went into the dining room and poked around behind the draperies, under the big walnut table with a floor-length embroidered table cloth covering most of it. Behind the china closet was another likely hiding place, but it proved empty.

That left the kitchen and the pantry. And the cellar. It was all kind of like a kid's game of hide-and-go-seek; they were looking for somebody who knew they were looking for him, and the object of the game was to tag him before he could break for freedom. The only difference was that all the players had guns, and if Harris was in the house, somebody was like as not going to get very dead in the next few minutes.

There was a deal table in the kitchen, the boards white with use and with scrubbing, although it was almost a sure thing that most of the meals in this house came from the cafe down the street. Nobody would have a lot of time for cooking.

The stove was cold, and nobody was in the space behind it. There was nobody under the table or back of the pie cabinet. The windows were open against the heat, because they were on the shady side of the house. Pearse looked out and saw Colonel standing in the alley. His Colt was in its holster, and he held his Winchester cradled in the crook of his left arm. Pearse guessed he'd do about as well with that as he would have with a pistol.

Carrington nudged him and pointed to the pantry. The door

was half open, and he could see shelves with sacks of flour and rice and potatoes and canned goods on them. The potatoes struck a wrong note. In a normal household, they would have been in the cellar, along with the carrots and turnips. But they were up in the pantry too. More wrong notes.

Carrington edged over to where he could see through the crack between the door and the frame. Pearse watched. Carrington wasn't satisfied. He stood to one side of the door-frame and kicked the door. It slammed flat against the wall, and then he went in. He poked at the vegetables and raised his eyebrows.

Pearse mouthed the word "cellar," and Carrington nodded.

Sometimes a house had a full cellar where stuff that should have been thrown out was stored. Sometimes the entrance was through an outside door, slanted to shed the rain. But a lot of times it was only a little hole in the ground you entered through a trapdoor.

There wouldn't be much of anything to store in this house, Pearse guessed, and there wasn't even an attic to store it in. He had seen the slant of the roof from the downstairs hall, but he motioned Carrington over and asked him anyway.

"No attic," Carrington muttered. "Just a little crawl space under the center, and I looked up there."

"No sign of him at all?"

Carrington shrugged. "No clothes lying around, if that's what you mean. No cigar butts."

Pearse poked his head out the window again to satisfy his curiosity. There was no slanting cellar door. There had to be a trapdoor somewhere in here.

They lifted rugs in the kitchen and the dining room and the parlor, and they finally found it in a corner of the pantry. The boards had been laid the way they normally would, not cut square to fit the hole. Somebody had taken a lot of trouble to conceal the trap. If it hadn't been for the note, they might have overlooked it.

Pearse guessed that was why the vegetables had been kept in the pantry. Somebody had wanted a searcher to think they were there because there was no cellar.

He pulled out his belt knife and pried up the trap, and he tried not to think about how a forty-five slug could go right through a floorboard with no trouble at all. Or maybe Harris was waiting to get a shot at whoever poked his head through the hole.

The air coming up was cool and damp, and it was kind of refreshing on a hot morning. Pearse could see wooden shelves along the side across from him: that wall was lined with stone, and there was a ledge on top of which the shelving had been built.

Carrington touched him on the shoulder. "Wait," he mouthed. He went back into the kitchen, and when he came back, he was holding a cheap, wooden-framed mirror that had hung over the sink. Pearse took it from him and held it so they could see into the cellar without exposing themselves.

For the first moment he expected to see the mirror shatter as a slug hit it, but nothing happened. It wasn't a large cellar, but he couldn't see all the way into the corners. There wasn't enough light.

He gave the mirror to Carrington and went back into the kitchen. There was a coal oil lamp on the table, and he lit it and came back. He poked it down the hole while Carrington held the mirror and looked. Carrington began to smile, and he gave Pearse the mirror while he held the lamp.

A pair of large green eyes above a neckerchief gag signalled frantically to him. A mop of auburn hair was all he needed to know that they had found Mary Lou Reilly.

Pearse climbed down the little ladder propped against the wall and went over to her. She had been tied hand and foot and gagged, but other than that she seemed all right. A plate and a fork were on the shelf near her, and the remains of a meal. Judging from what was left, she had eaten bread and saltpork and drunk water. Fat Gertie wasn't going to waste good money feeding a hostage.

Pearse spoke low, just in case sound carried in the house. "We're going to take you to a safe place. When I take that gag off, I want you to be real quiet. I don't want anybody in the house to know we let you out. All right?"

She nodded emphatically, and Pearse went to work. His belt knife made short work of the rope that bound her arms and legs, and then he untied the gag while she flexed her limbs to get back circulation.

He let her climb the ladder ahead of him so Carrington could help her up, and then the three of us stood grinning at each other in triumph.

For a little bit, they even forgot about Harris.

Chapter Eighteen

Carrington was the first of them to come back to earth. "We'll just hold what we got," he said in a low voice. "Take her back to my house. Just walk out the front door when I tell Gertie they all can come downstairs. Go west to the cross street and turn north. My missus knows she was missing, so she'll be glad to keep her until we get rid of Harris."

Mary Lou remembered something. "I'm a deputy marshal, Sheriff. I need a gun."

Carrington nodded. "My missus has two in the house. Tell her I said to give you one."

They made it out the front door without a hitch. Inside she could hear Carrington bawling for the ladies to come down, and when they heard the tramp of feet on the stairs, they walked down the street.

She told Pearse about what had happened to her. "I sure wished you or Colonel had been around, Charlie."

"I wish we had too," Pearse said. "I thought it was safe enough out at Jim's place, but somebody must have talked."

"He didn't hurt me or anything. But he chloroformed me, and when I came to, I was at that place. He told Gertie he'd pay her fifty dollars a day to keep me. Then they stuck me in that damn cellar. Three times a day one of the women came down and fed me and that was about it. Nobody talked to me or anything. I guess she didn't trust any of her girls."

There was no sign of Harris. If she'd had a gun, she'd have felt better about it, but she didn't. If Harris showed up before they got to the sheriff's house, she hoped Charlie would be a match for him.

Mrs. Carrington hurried them inside. "I suppose that old fool knows what he's doing," she said. Mary Lou realized that she was being affectionate in the way that wives of lawmen often are. She might call him an old fool, but she'd scratch the eyes out of anyone else who did.

"The sheriff said you'd have a gun for me."

Mrs. Carrington smiled. "He told me you got deputized by that Marshal Clinton. I got a nice Navy Colt you can keep for now. Sheriff keeps two of them handy in case of trouble. I'll hang on to one and you can have the other."

Mary Lou was satisfied. She had expected a problem with the gun, and there hadn't been any. Mrs. Carrington was no stranger to guns. Or to trouble either.

Pearse cleared his throat. "It's probably safe enough," he said. "But just in case. Each of you ought to keep a gun on you at all times. And don't be bashful about using it. This Harris is about as evil as they come."

"I've handled a gun before, young man," Mrs. Carrington said. "And from what Sheriff's told me, so has this young lady."

When Pearse got back to Fat Gertie's, Carrington was waiting for him on the front porch. "Nothing's happened yet," he said. "I told Colonel we'd got his girl safe and sound. You want to go around the west side, I'll take the east. We'll look in that shed and the outhouse, and then we'll have it nailed down."

Pearse nodded and set out. Harris might have learned that they'd searched the house and he wouldn't stay to be caught in a shed.

But they searched anyway. Colonel stayed in the alley with his Winchester, and the sheriff went up to the outhouse and kicked the door open, standing well to the side. Empty.

Pearse pushed Carrington out of the way and took the shed himself, kicking the door open with a resounding bang, and for a long moment they waited for something to happen. Nothing did, and Carrington covered him while he went in.

He ducked around the door frame quickly to get out of the light, and his gun searched the shadows for movement. Gradually he made out the shape of an old buggy, a barrel that had once contained flour, and stray bits of harness and hardware. A little late in the day, he looked up at the rafters. Nothing lurked there.

No Harris.

They joined forces in the alley. Colonel was maybe more impatient than the others, because he was anxious to see Mary Lou; but he agreed with Carrington that it would be dangerous for him to go to her. "Gertie's going to tell Harris we've got her, though. And Harris is smart enough to figure out where you put her."

"How's Gertie going to get word to him?" Pearse asked.

"Easy," Carrington said. "They've got something worked out by now. She'll probably send one of the girls down the street on an errand, and the girl'll leave word for him. Maybe at the hardware store. Maybe at one of the saloons."

"Well, what can we do about it?" Pearse asked.

"I suggest we go on down to the cafe and have us some dinner and talk over the situation," Carrington said. "There ain't a lot we can do until we know more."

Coffee and food brightened up the afternoon, not that it needed it. The sun was already heating up the boards on the walks and the siding on the buildings, and the glare outside was enough to make them squint when they looked out the window. But it was cool enough inside the cafe as yet, and the dim light was a blessing.

"Harris won't come back for Mary Lou," Carrington guessed. "What he's after is the money. You got that in a safe place, Colonel?"

"Safe enough. It ain't in the bank, but it's where he won't find it." He sipped at his coffee. "But you're wrong about Mary Lou. He's got a hate for me that won't quit. If he can hurt her and kill me and get the money too, he'll be in hog heaven. He'll settle for the money and a ride out of town, but sooner or later he's going to come after me and Mary Lou. I'd bet my bottom dollar on it."

"Can you scare up another deputy, Sheriff?" Pearse asked. "There's only the three of us."

"Kind of hard to find deputies right after one of them got his neck broke, Charlie. Makes some fellers a little shy, if you take my meaning."

A fly buzzed noisily above the remains of the meal. Dishes clattered in the kitchen, and someone scraped an iron pot with a steel spoon. Some folks lived normal lives, Pearse thought.

Carrington broke the silence. "Any suggestions?"

"So far, he's free as a bird," Colonel said. "He might just get out of town and wait for a better time. I doubt it though. The thing about Lieutenant Harris is, he's impatient. He'll try to get to me to get hold of the money."

"And maybe he'll try to find Mary Lou to get some leverage," Pearse said. "I can't see him going up against your men, Colonel. They know all about him, and they'll be on their guard."

"I ought to go back to the sheriff's house to guard Mary Lou," Colonel said. "That way, he's got two targets in one."

Carrington objected. "If I go back home, it'll look like I come home for a late dinner. If anybody else goes, Harris'll know she's in there."

They split up. Colonel went back to the stable to wait for Harris to get in touch with him, Carrington went home to check on Mary Lou and Mrs. Carrington, and Pearse agreed to roam around.

The first place he went was to the alley behind Gertie's. He wanted to see if Gertie would try to get word to Harris that she no longer had Mary Lou.

It was possible that Gertie would simply send one of her girls out the front door, but he didn't think so. He didn't even think twice about Gertie not knowing Mary Lou was no longer there. She was too cagey not to have checked the cellar as soon as they had left. And it was in her nature to send somebody out the back way to get a message to Harris.

He waited between a couple of outbuildings for a while. The flies found out where he was and came buzzing around, but he tried to ignore them, and after awhile a woman came walking down the alley.

It was the same woman who had passed him the note about the cellar. Pearse let her pass and counted to twenty, and then he followed her, keeping pretty well out of sight. It wasn't hard: she didn't look back once. She ducked between the Red Dog and Kelly's, and he followed. She turned right when she came to the street, and he got there just in time to see her going through the batwing doors of Kelly's.

Pearse went in after her. She sat herself down at a table, and the bartender came over with a shot glass without even asking her what she wanted. Pearse guessed she was a regular there. He called for a beer and went over to the table. "Mind if I sit down?" Without waiting, he pulled out a chair.

"It's a free country, Mr. Pearse."

So she knew his name. He had no doubt but that she'd pass that information along as soon as she got the chance. "I wanted to thank you for the note."

She smiled. "I don't know what you're talking about."

"I'd bet you got another note. Maybe it's not for me."

"You could be right," she said. "But then, you could be wrong."

He fished in his pocket and came up with a five-dollar gold piece. "Would this be enough to let me read it? Always supposing there was one?"

"That says there's a note. It's going to need some company before anybody gets to read it."

He grinned. "Information's pretty hard to come by." He fished in his pocket again and came up with another five dollars.

The second gold piece followed the first into her reticule. Out of sight, out of mind, he thought.

Her hand slid over his leg, found his hand. He glanced at the paper she held onto. "The gril is gone, took by the sherrif."

That said enough to put Harris up to date. "Who do you give this to?" Pearse asked.

"I don't. I leave it on the table and walk out."

Pearse thanked her, finished his beer and left. Maybe somebody could watch Kelly's for the rest of the day and see who came to collect the note or who went out to deliver it, but Pearse had a feeling it wouldn't do a lot of good. Harris was smart enough to stay away from the saloons, and any messenger he might use could be any of the patrons of Kelly's, and it would be hard to know which one.

For another thing, it was possible that Harris already knew about the "gril" and that he was already taking steps to get her back, if that was what he had in mind.

Pearse considered walking back to Carrington's house and checking in with him, and then he abandoned the idea. Carrington and his wife and Mary Lou were all armed, and Harris wouldn't be fool enough to go there and try to seize the girl when he could go after Colonel.

If Harris made a move at all in daylight, it would be against Colonel. Once he had the money, he could take his own sweet time to get revenge. If Pearse guessed right, Harris would be staying at Gertie's nights and holing up somewhere else during the day, maybe in one of the rooms over one of the saloons. One thing was certain: he wouldn't be roaming around the streets looking for Pearse or Carrington.

Pearse turned down the street toward the livery stable. If Harris had contacted Colonel, it was time he found out about it.

Josh was standing in the open door, watching the street bake in the sun. He had an old Colt Police model five-shot stuck in his hip pocket. At least he was prepared, although Pearse didn't know how he was going to get his gun out in time to do him any good. Hip-pocket draws had to be the slowest of them all.

"Been here all along?" Pearse asked.

"Went across to the cafe for a cup of coffee, but I watched the door all the time."

Why hadn't he gone in back to Colonel's office? There was usually a pot on the stove.

But Pearse only asked if Colonel was in.

"He was back in his office a while back, Charlie. Pete's watching the back door."

Pearse wondered if Josh was the one who had let slip that Colonel had sent somebody up to Deadwood, but he said nothing beyond thanking the man.

He went through the big barn, past the rows of horses, each in its stall, past the harness and saddlery hanging from pegs. There was a good smell of hay and horses and saddle-soaped leather—the signs of a well-run stable.

There was no sign of Pete. Pearse hesitated a moment and

then stepped to the side of the runway. Pete should have been standing in the door or near it, if he was to do any good. As an old army man, Colonel would have told him what to do and where to do it. Of course he could be out in the pen working with a horse or cleaning up, but Pearse couldn't count on it. The difference between staying alive and dying often hinged on little things like making easy assumptions.

Pearse could see the horses in the catch pen through the door. They were moving about, as if somebody had been recently among them.

The office door was just ahead and to the left. Pearse cradled the Sharps in the crook of his left arm and drew the big Starr revolver, and then he went ahead. There was no sound from the office, and he stopped just short of the door frame and listened.

There was no sound but the buzzing of flies from one of the empty stalls, and there was no familiar reek of cigar smoke either. And then he heard a familiar noise from the catch pen. Somebody was saddling a horse.

He took a quick peek through the doorway to make sure nobody was in the office, and then he went forward to the big rear door and hugged the door post. A boot stuck out on the right side, and when Pearse risked a look, he saw Pete stretched out on the ground. He had a bad cut on his head, and the flies were busy with it. Pearse could see the slow rise and fall of his chest, so he wasn't dead, but he was going to need help soon.

Harris had gotten to Pete, maybe to Colonel as well, and he was somewhere near. Unless it had been Colonel saddling a horse. No. Colonel wouldn't have left Pete lying there.

Harris was very near. Pearse could feel it. And where was Colonel?

Pearse backed into the gloom of the stable and watched the catch pen. A horse was being led out. It was saddled, and there were saddlebags and a scabbard with what looked to be a Springfield carbine was strapped to the saddle. Colonel was leading the horse. He was having a time of it, because he walked like a man who was hurting. There was a large bruise on the side of his face, and his hands were bound behind his back. He had no boots on, and his stocking feet were red.

Harris had tortured him, that was plain. But where was Harris? Behind Pearse in the stable somewhere? No; Harris had saddled the horse and made Colonel stay with him until he was done. That way, Colonel couldn't call for help until Harris was well on his way.

Pearse backed into the office. Nobody could come up behind him there. He listened to the plop of hooves on the soft dirt and the rasp of Colonel's breathing as he held in the pain of his tortured feet.

"Close enough," Harris said just outside the big door. "Now you can go inside and sit down, Sergeant. And I'll be seeing you later."

"You got your money, Harris. Now, for God's sake, go and leave us alone."

"For a while. When I have time, I'll come visit you again."

Pearse watched through a crack as Harris took his time about mounting. Now was the time to take him, now that he was occupied with the horse. But Pearse waited.

Colonel hobbled through the door and came staggering down the runway, probably headed for Josh. He was mumbling as he went, and he lurched to the side and leaned against a stall. And Harris yelled.

The horse bolted straight down the runway, and as it passed, Pearse could see the pistol in Harris's hand. And Pearse moved.

"Hold it!" he yelled. But of course Harris wasn't stopping for anybody. He hauled in on the reins and turned the horse back toward Colonel and toward Pearse, and the big Army Colt flashed and banged in the confines of the stable, and Pearse heard the thud as the slug hit the doorpost beside him.

Pearse could see it all, and all of it at once, the way he did when things were happening fast. It was as if time stood almost still for a long moment, and there was plenty of time to do what needed doing, because everything else was moving so slowly.

Harris leveled his gun hand, and then Pearse fired and the horse reared. Pearse fired again at the red stain on Harris's shirt, and then he emptied the other four chambers of the Starr into Harris's body as he was falling from the saddle.

The horse drug Harris a little way, and then his foot slid out of the stirrup and the horse kept going into the catch pen and safety. Josh had finally gotten his old Colt out of his pocket, and he came running up.

"It's over," Pearse said. "Better see to Pete. He's out there, and he's in a bad way."

He walked over to Harris and picked up his gun. Just to be on the safe side, he took the deringer out of his boot, but it was plain to see that Mr. Harris wasn't going anywhere any more. A dinner plate could have covered the holes in his chest. His eyes were slightly open, and his mouth showed white teeth as if he'd found something to laugh at, at the end.

Pearse went over to Colonel and helped him into his office. He sat him in his chair and propped his feet on the other chair, and then he searched the desk until he found the whiskey and poured a generous helping for Colonel.

Colonel clutched the thick glass with both hands and swallowed. He winced when the raw liquor hit his battered lips, but he drank anyway.

"I owe you another one, Charlie," he mumbled, and then he passed out cold.

Chapter Nineteen

With Josh's help, Pearse got Colonel and Pete loaded in a buck-board, and then he went to the catch pen and unsaddled the horse Harris had ridden. He took the sack containing the money out of the saddlebag where Harris had put it, while Josh caught up a gentle old-timer whose time had almost come and hitched it to the buggy.

After that, he drove down the street to the doctor's office and called on him for help. And then he drove down to Carrington's house to give him the news.

"Did you tell Clinton?" the sheriff wanted to know.

"I figured that was something that could wait until we talked."

"Let's get on down to the office then. We'll go over it down there, and we'll take Miss Reilly down to Doc's to visit with Colonel."

Before they left, Mary Lou turned over her gun to the Sheriff's wife. "I'll be eternally grateful that I didn't have to use this," she said.

"Would you have?" Mrs. Carrington asked.

Mary Lou grinned. "Oh, yes. I certainly would have."

By the time they got back to the doctor's, Colonel's feet had been washed and bound in clean linen, and Doc was working on his mouth. Harris had slashed his feet with a knife, but Doc said they'd heal, if he didn't get poisoned. He'd washed them with alcohol, just to make sure.

Pete was out for the count, but Doc said it was a mercy, because he could stitch up the cut in his head while he was unconscious and he wouldn't feel a thing.

Clinton wasn't too happy. "Couldn't you take him alive, Charlie? Wasn't there some way we could have brought him to trial?"

"None that I know of, Marshal."

Carrington gave Pearse a look that said he didn't believe him, but he didn't have enough to go on to say so right out.

Mary Lou and Colonel were lost in a world of their own.

The sheriff and Pearse wished Clinton and Colonel a speedy recovery, and then they went out together. They took the buckboard down to the stable and turned it over to Josh.

Harris's body lay in the runway the way Pearse had left it, and the sheriff examined it. "Leave it for Doc," he said when he'd finished. "He's got to look at it and make out a coroner's report, and then we can get it underground."

"Better be soon," Pearse said. "It's mighty hot."

Doc would look at it and say that Harris had died of six gunshot wounds through the torso. The undertaker would come down with his black hearse and embalm it, and when he got Harris cleaned up a little, he'd probably strap him to a board and display him in his window for the school-kids and other curious folk to look at. It was supposed to be a good example of what happened to sidewinders who broke the law. Pearse guessed that maybe it was.

He and Carrington walked the length of the street in silence. There was plenty to talk about, but it could wait for the privacy of the sheriff's office. Carrington unlocked the door and opened the one window. He sat down behind his desk and Pearse took the other chair.

"Seems to me like we done this before, Charlie," Carrington said. "Suppose you tell me what happened down there. The truth, not what I'm going to have to write down."

"What makes you think there's two different ways of telling it, Sheriff?"

"For openers, you knew where Harris was before he even knew you was there. The way you told it down to the stable, he stopped to get on his horse. Now he probably had a gun on Colonel, although it's kind of hard to mount a horse and hold a gun on somebody at the same time. But let's say he had a gun. You were behind cover, you could have called on him to drop it. But you didn't. Why?"

He had hesitated. He could have called out to Harris, but he hadn't. "I don't know. The horse was between him and me when he mounted, and he had cover."

"That's true. And then he might have got a shot at you over the horse. But what we're left with is, you let him get mounted and then you let him come in to ride Colonel down or shoot him or scare him to death. You even let him get in a shot at you, and then when you couldn't miss, you shot him out of the saddle."

"It was him or me."

"That's what it comes down to in the end, don't it? But I'm going to suggest that there's another way of looking at it. You could have figured out in your own mind that it would be hard for a jury to convict Harris for two murders, when there were no witnesses. And if he'd got acquitted here, then he could have got acquitted up in Deadwood, too, because there were no witnesses up there either, once Murphy was dead."

Pearse stared at him. "You're saying you think I took the law in my own hands?"

"Maybe. You might have done that, you might not. I don't honestly know. It wouldn't be the first time a lawman had done just that."

"I did what I figured I had to do, and that's about the size of it. He wasn't in cover when I shot him, I can tell you that much. I let him turn his horse after I told him to halt, and he could see me plain as I could see him. And the holes in him are all in the front."

"There's that," the sheriff admitted. "And there's a hole in the doorpost where he shot at you and missed."

Pearse fished in his pocket for a cheroot. "I don't see the problem then. No matter how you cut it, it was self-defense."

"The problem is, Charlie, I'm seeing a bright young fellow who's maybe getting to think he can help out the judges by taking care of the sidewinders before they come to trial and waste everybody's time and patience. Country's changing, boy, and if you keep on with this, one of these days you're going to find yourself up against a murder charge. And you're going to be no better than the man you killed."

Pearse started to answer him, and then he stopped. He didn't know. He thought he'd done the right thing, but Carrington had raised doubts in his mind.

"Don't know which it was, huh? I'd do some thinking about it, if I was you. I'm not saying you was right, and I'm not saying you was wrong. What I'm saying is, you better figure out in your own mind just what made you pop your caps on Harris before you get in too deep to get back out."

When Carrington was done, Pearse walked back to the hotel to clean up and change clothes for the night's game. It was time to make a living, doing what he did best: poker.

Marshal Clinton was up and about two days after that. Doc had told him that he was healing nicely, so he took it to heart and came down the main drag to explore the mysteries of Julesburg.

He also wanted to get back the deputy's badges he'd pinned on Mary Lou and Pearse. "They cost the government money, Charlie," he said. "Got to have 'em back."

Pearse handed over his badge. For a change he wasn't anybody's deputy. Carrington had taken the deputy sheriff's badge back as soon as he learned that Clinton would recover. "You'll have to talk to Mrs. Colonel Reynolds about the other one," he told Carrington.

"I heard tell Mary Lou and Colonel tied the knot. Hadn't been for you, it wouldn't have happened."

Pearse shrugged. "It might have. Harris had the money, and all he had in mind right then was getting out of town with a whole skin. He might have forgotten all about revenge after that."

"You and I know that's a bunch of horse apples, Charlie. A man like Harris lives to kill people. Robbery's only a kind of sideline when there ain't anybody handy to kill."

"Carrington seems to think I took the law in my own hands and made an honest man out of Harris the wrong way."

Clinton shrugged. "That's for you to figure out for yourself, Charlie. The way I see it, you didn't have a lot of choice in the matter."

"He figured I could have taken Harris prisoner if I'd called him while he was mounting his horse."

"Maybe you could have. I don't know, I wasn't there. But sometimes it's mighty hard to act the right way when you know lives are at stake, especially when one of them is your own. You don't have time to think, you got to act."

Pearse said nothing. He had all the answer he wanted. There hadn't been time to think about the right or wrong of it when Harris made his final play. He had been riding to hurt Colonel again, to whip him of his manhood, and Pearse had stopped him. He hadn't thought of cheating the hangman, he hadn't held any personal grudge.

In his books, that made it right.

"I see you thought it over some," Clinton said.

Pearse nodded. "After what Carrington said, I'd have to be a fool not to."

Dick Martin came over to Pearse's table with two beers. "Hot weather calls for something to cut the thirst," he said. "On the house, Charlie."

He went back behind the bar, where the usual lithograph of Custer's Last Stand had supplanted Odalisque. Personally, Pearse preferred naked ladies to gory battle scenes. He watched Dick polish a glass, and it came to him that he'd better remember the scene. In a few short years, it might be gone for good.

"Anything you figure you might have done different?" Clinton asked.

Pearse shook his head. "I don't think I did anything wrong there. I don't even think Carrington believes that. I think he was telling me in his own way to make sure of why I was doing something before I did it."

"He's a pretty smart old coon," Clinton said. "He's a good lawman, and he's mighty careful about what he does, which is a good way to be. But there's times you can't be too careful. Man can get killed that way."

"It's a funny thing, but when the chips are down everything

seems like it's moving in slow motion. You think you got all the time in the world, and of course you haven't, it only seems that way. Why didn't I call him while he was getting in the saddle? I don't know. I guess I wanted to make sure he wouldn't grab Colonel and use him as a shield. But I don't know. The only thing I do know was, I had to stop him when I could do it without getting my head blown off. I did what I had to do."

Clinton took a long drag at his beer. "That's good enough for me, Charlie. In the end, that's all that counts. Now I got a little proposition for you. Want to hear it?"

"I'm listening."

"I had a telegram from Deadwood yesterday. Tom Henry and Alois Krause quit. I'm going to need a deputy on a permanent basis. Maybe two. You want to apply for the job?"

Pearse lit a cheroot. There was nothing much in Julesburg for him any more. He didn't have to be a genius to figure that out. Carrington would go to his deathbed wondering if he had been a good lawman or a murderer. And Julesburg was getting old. In another ten years it would be another tamed prairie town, stodgy and sedate, wanting nothing but peace and prosperity.

It might be all right for Colonel and his lady, married and respectable and maybe raising a family and getting rich. But there would be nothing for Pearse but sitting at a round poker table, getting fat and complacent.

"Count me in, Marshal," he said. "When do I start?"

WAKE THE HOLLOW
BY GABY TRIANA

Forget the ghosts, Mica. It's real, live people you should fear.

Tragedy has brought Micaela Burgos back to her hometown of
Sleepy Hollow. It's been six years since she chose to live with
her father in Miami instead of her eccentric mother. And now
her mother is dead.

This town will suck you in and not let go.

Sleepy Hollow may be famous for its fabled headless horseman,
but the town is real. So are its prejudices and hatred, targeting
Mica's family as outsiders. But ghostly voices carry on the wind,
whispering that her mother's death was based on hate...not an
accident at all. With the help of two very different guys—who pull
at her heart in very different ways—Micaela must awaken the
hidden secret of Sleepy Hollow...before she meets her mother's
fate.

Find the answers.

Unless, of course, the answers find you first.